D1094134

Who Goes Home?

Who Goes Home?

Elizabeth Lemarchand

Walker and Company
New York

First published in the United States of America
in 1987 by the Walker Publishing Company, Inc.

Library of Congress Cataloging-in-Publication Data

Lemarchand, Elizabeth.
   Who goes home?

   I. Title.
PR6062.E5W5   1987   823'.914   87-6181
ISBN 0-8027-5675-1

Printed in the United States of America

10 9 8 7 6 5 4 3 2 1

Chief Characters

The Anstey Family
John Anstey (deceased)
Paul Anstey and Hugh Anstey, his sons
Martin Anstey (Hugh's son)

Maynard Hooper, landlord of the Peatcutters Inn at Dollaford
Gemma Ford, his niece by marriage
Joan Venner, a resident of Dollaford
Mabel Pettinger, proprietor of *Dogdays*, boarding kennels near Dollaford
Brian Moss, one of her helpers
Detective-Superintendent Bainbridge and Detective-Inspector Parkin of the Highcastle CID
Detective-Chief Superintendent Tom Pollard and Detective-Inspector Gregory Toye of New Scotland Yard

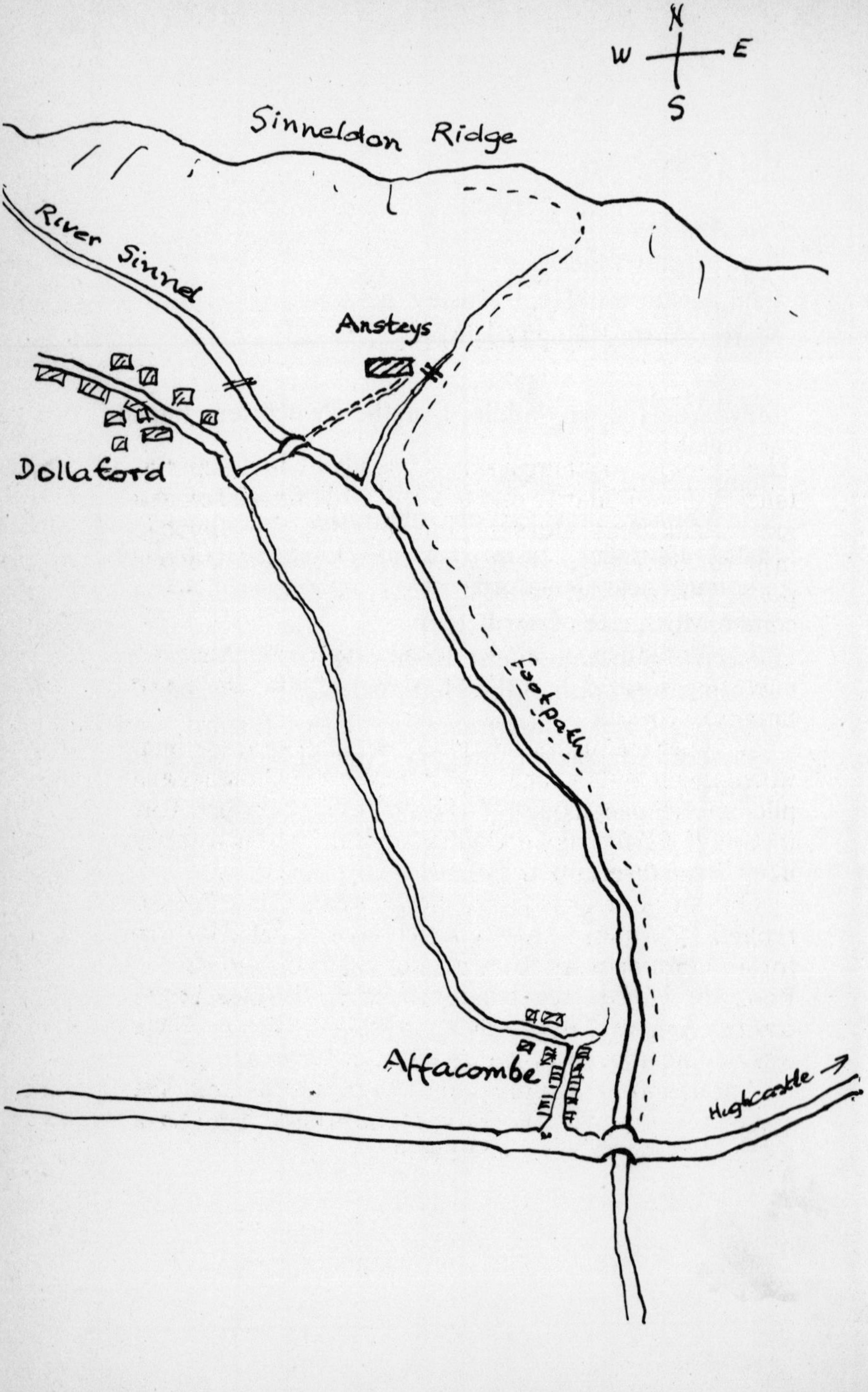
N
W
E
S
Sinneldon Ridge
River Sinnel
Ansteys
Dollaford
Footpath
Affacombe
Highcastle →

Chapter 1

'Here, hold everything a sec.' Detective-Chief Superintendent Tom Pollard came to a halt and subsided on to a grassy bank at the side of the track. He began to rummage in his rucksack. 'We'd better have a look at the map at this point. Olivia said it was easy to overshoot the top of the combe which leads down.'

Jane Pollard sank on to the bank beside her husband and they studied a 1:50,000 sheet of the Ordnance Survey.

'We must be just here,' she said, jabbing at the map with a finger and turning to glance over her shoulder at a pile of Cyclopaean boulders behind them. 'Grouch Tor, it's called. Perfect name, don't you think? It looks exactly like a huge disgruntled animal.'

'One of your artistic reactions, love,' Tom Pollard replied. 'My guess is that "Grouch" is a mangled version for some Saxon word for a heap of ruddy old stones . . . Look,' he went on, reverting to the map, 'this must be the combe; roughly halfway down there's the house Olivia was talking about – Anstey's Farm, it's called.'

'About another couple of miles,' Jane estimated. She glanced at her watch. 'We've got time in hand. Let's have a short break. This is a good spot.'

1

They sprawled contentedly on grass and heather.

A week's leave at the end of one of Pollard's cases had led to an invitation from Olivia Strode, an old friend who lived in the village of Affacombe below the eastern edge of Crownmoor. Olivia's son David and daughter-in-law, Wimbledon friends and near neighbours of Tom and Jane, had offered to take in the Pollard's twin son and daughter, contemporaries of their own two children, a scheme greeted with enthusiasm by the quartet. From conversations over the telephone it was clear that a good time was being had by all in perfect June weather.

On this Friday, the last day of their holiday, Olivia Strode had driven Pollard and Jane to a point twelve miles to the north of Affacombe. Here she had dropped them with picnic lunches to walk back to the village along the crest of Sinneldon, the eastern bastion of Crownmoor.

'About three miles short of the village there's a combe running down to the Sinnel,' she had told them, 'and a rather pleasant path all the way back along the river bank if you feel like a different landscape at that stage.'

Presently Jane looked at her watch. 'I suppose we ought to press on,' she said reluctantly.

Pollard gave a resigned assenting grunt and they got to their feet. Ahead of them the grassy track rose and fell gently, snaking its way through young green bracken and dark dead gorse. Tiny white saxifrage flowered in the crevices of granite outcrops. There was an occasional vivid splash of early bell heather and at intervals a prolific scatter of tiny golden rock roses. The Pollards were good walkers and swung along easily in their shorts and open-necked shirts. At intervals they stopped to gaze at the spectacular panorama to the south. Here the lower land beyond the Sinnel had been farmed down the centuries. It was an immense patchwork quilt of fields of an endless variety of shapes and colours: golden yellow, strong red

2

and dusty pink, greens of subtly different shades. Here and there dark patches of woodland introduced emphatic notes, and on the far horizon was the shimmer of the sea.

Eventually a few stunted hawthorns took shape in the distance, and along the track were the traces of long abandoned fields. Five minutes later the Pollards stood looking down into a steep combe followed by a tumbling stream and a stony path. They picked their way with some care in the unaccustomed gloom of close-packed dwarf birch, rowans and hawthorns. Blinking as they emerged into the light they looked down at the combe opening out ahead of them with a sudden reduction of its gradient. Some distance ahead a footbridge crossed the stream, and on the far side on a natural terrace well above flood level was a low rectangular granite house with green shuttered windows.

A few yards further on Pollard stopped dead.

'Look,' he said. 'Somebody coming up from the road.'

Impelled by a sudden unspoken impulse they dropped down in the lee of some bushes and watched the approaching figure.

'It's a male,' Jane said. 'You can always tell by the walk. Men somehow push themselves forward with their shoulders. More conventionally dressed than us.'

As they watched, the figure became clearly identifiable as a youngish man in a light suit who stopped short of the house and subjected it to prolonged scrutiny. He then went up to the front door and appeared to knock. There was no response and he tried again with the same result. He then made an apparently unsuccessful attempt to peer through the shuttered windows, and finally went round to the back of the house and disappeared from view.

'So what?' Jane queried when a couple of minutes had passed. 'If only we were a bit higher up we could see over the roof.'

As she spoke the caller became visible again, apparently investigating the outbuildings in the rear of the house.

'Perhaps we should make our presence felt,' Pollard said thoughtfully.

'No way!' Jane retorted. 'We're on holiday, and if you tell me police are always on duty I'll leave you . . . Look, he's giving up . . .'

As she spoke the young man reappeared. After a final look at the front of the house he went off down the combe towards the main road. The Pollards sat listening. After a few minutes there came a distant sound of a car engine being started up. Pollard got to his feet.

'Come on,' he said. 'Let's go and have a snoop ourselves.'

They followed the path down to the footbridge, crossed the stream and stood contemplating the building.

'Interesting,' he commented. 'It's an original Crownmoor long-house. That slightly different bit at the end would have been the shippon, and I expect there's a cross-passage behind the front door. The first floor's a later addition.'

'Decidedly remote and primitive,' Jane said. 'No electricity cables or telephone line. How do you suppose they manage for water and drains?'

On further investigation they found the farmhouse very securely locked and shuttered. In the open space behind it was a well with a padlocked cover and signs of a pipe having been laid to a pump outside the back door of the house. Nearer the stream was a septic tank. Pollard sniffed at the door of a shed and diagnosed a paraffin store. Tyre tracks led to and from another shed which was apparently used as a garage.

'Well, they've got the basics,' he said, 'but it must be pretty grim in the winter.'

Jane asked how there could ever have been a viable farm in the combe.

'It must have been pretty marginal farming. Summer grazing up on the moor, and winter fodder grown in those abandoned fields we saw and fed to the stock in the shippon. A tough life: no EEC handouts in those days.'

A rutted and partly grass-grown track wide enough to take a car led down the combe. It crossed the Sinnel by a primitive low bridge to join the road which linked Affacombe to the other villages along the river. The Pollards kept to the path on the left bank recommended by Olivia Strode, enjoying the cool of early evening and the quietly running water. Eventually they arrived at Poldens, a little stiff and footsore but announcing that they had had an absolutely super day.

Later, bathed and changed, they relaxed over pre-supper drinks in Olivia's sitting room-cum-study. Glancing around, Pollard was briefly transported back to the day, not far short of sixteen years earlier, when he had seen the room for the first time in the course of his Affacombe murder investigation. There were even more books now that Olivia had become a recognised local historian. The photographs included her son David's wedding group and a chronological record of Rupert and Ursula, their children. The fine old picture-map of the county which had featured so oddly in one of his waking dreams still hung over the mantelpiece. . . . It had been a winter afternoon with a bright fire on the hearth. He could remember exactly where he had been sitting when Olivia unconsciously let fall that vital clue to the murderer's identity . . .

He surfaced to hear Jane asking about Anstey's Farm.

'Do people actually live there?'

'It belongs to a man called Paul Anstey who comes down for a few days from time to time. He's a London

5

businessman and owns a travel agency, I've heard,' Olivia replied.

'Originally a Crownmoor long-house, I take it?' Pollard enquired.

'Yes. The original structure's quite recognisable, isn't it, in spite of all the later additions? According to hearsay the Anstey family came from up-country somewhere and bought the house from its emigrating owners. Long before our time, of course. In the middle of the last century, I've been told. They partly rebuilt it and settled there, doing a bit of farming at first. When my John bought this cottage in 1937, an old John Anstey was living at the farm. He was more or less a recluse and said to have lost most of his money. Paul Anstey's his son. He's about sixty, I should say. He was pointed out to me once, but I've never met him socially. You see, he's Dollaford-based for what local contacts he has. It's nearer the farm than Affacombe, and has a much more with-it pub. A new man called Hooper bought it about five years ago and seems to be turning it into an "in" place – sorry, no pun intended – for Polharbour people to drive out to for dinner. Have another drink, both of you.'

'There was a caller at Anstey's Farm this afternoon,' Pollard remarked, sitting down again after refilling their glasses. 'A youngish man, who left his car down on the road and walked up to the house. He knocked twice, and when it was obvious the place was shut up he tried to peer through the shutters, and then went round to have a good look at the back premises. We were watching from higher up on the opposite side of the valley. In the end he called it a day and went off again.'

'Perhaps a London friend dropping in on chance,' Olivia said. 'I expect he brings friends down on some of his visits. Come along to the kitchen and bring your drinks: you must be starving after that walk. I've only got

6

to get a casserole out of the oven.'

The next morning the Pollards left early by car for Wimbledon. Olivia Strode waved them off from the step of Poldens.

Pollard glanced back and gave her a parting salute.

'Wearing amazingly well, isn't she?' he remarked to Jane. 'Grey now, of course, but still the same nice little round-about figure and brisk walk, and that shrewd sensible face.'

'It think she's terrific for seventy-four,' Jane replied. 'Definitely the top of your list of case friendships.'

Chapter 2

The young man in the light suit whose abortive call at
Anstey's Farm had interested the Pollards was Martin
Anstey, the only child of Hugh, old John Anstey's
younger son. After serving in the army during the
1939–1945 war Hugh had emigrated to Southern Rhodesia. He had made money as a tobacco grower and married
the daughter of British immigrants. Martin, born in 1954,
had above-average ability and won a major scholarship to
a South African university which he took up on complet-
ing his compulsory national service.

Hugh Anstey had always intended to return to England
on reaching retiring age, and with this in view had transferred money to his bank in London as long as this was
feasible. On his advice Martin stayed on in South Africa
after graduating, and joined the staff of the Cape Town
branch of Randall's, a well-known London publishing
house. Then suddenly, in 1982, Hugh and his wife were
both killed in an air crash. This tragedy decided Martin,
who was becoming progressively more disenchanted with
life in South Africa, to return to England on his own
account. His employers in Cape Town regretfully fixed up
a year's trial for him with the firm's head office in London
where he duly presented himself in the spring of 1984.

After settling into his new job which he liked from the start and finding a suitable small flat, he took stock. The future appeared quite promising. Now just on thirty, he was tall with rather untidy dark hair, intelligent eyes surveying the world through large horn-rimmed spectacles of a geometrical design, and strong features. His new colleagues liked him and he had no difficulty in making friends. These were predominantly male. Apart from a few fleeting affairs in South Africa he had so far taken only a limited interest in women. Thanks to his father's foresight he found himself with a useful private income as well as a good salary. With his immediate preoccupations resolved he debated the question of whether or not to attempt to contact his only known relative in England, his uncle Paul Anstey, to discuss the provisions of John Anstey's Will. Finally he decided to make an approach, and wrote to say that he would call in at Anstey's Farm during the afternoon of Friday, 15 June.

The situation was likely to be sticky. Hugh had kept in touch with his father after emigrating, and had received a notification of his death in 1960 from a Highcastle solicitor, followed in due course by a copy of his Will. The farmhouse and what little land remained had been left to Paul for his lifetime in trust for his eldest surviving son. If he died without legitimate issue it was to revert to Hugh, and ultimately to his eldest surviving son.

Hugh reacted angrily, having built up over the years an agreeable picture of spending his old age in his childhood home duly reconditioned and modernised. After Paul's treatment of his father it seemed hardly believable that he was to inherit a life interest in the farm. John Anstey had lost the greater part of his invested capital in the financial upheavals of the 1920s and early '30s following on the First World War. Paul had been removed from Marlchester at the age of sixteen, and instead of going on to

9

Cambridge as planned to read modern languages had been found a post in a London insurance office. His reaction had been to break off all contact with his father. The rupture was so complete and final that the solicitor who dealt with John's affairs had considerable difficulty in tracing him after his father's death in 1960. There had been no question of Marlchester for Hugh who was educated at Polharbour Grammar School, leaving at sixteen to work on a local farm. He joined the army in 1939, served throughout the war and emigrated to Southern Rhodesia in 1948, seeing little prospect of a promising future for himself in England, but always maintaining contact with his father and giving him financial help from time to time. His indignation over John Anstey's Will was understandable. He wrote curtly to Paul, stating that he had received a copy and would hold him responsible for the maintenance of the property. His letter was unanswered.

So too was Martin's, in which he had proposed a visit to Anstey's Farm on Friday, 15 June. Not particularly surprised, he decided to make the trip all the same. After the vast open spaces of southern Africa the tiny scale and endless variety of the English landscape fascinated him, and the prospect of seeing the surroundings of his father's early days had a particular appeal.

He left London by car early on the Friday morning, broke his journey at Highcastle and finally arrived at the turning up to Anstey's Farm in mid-afternoon. He parked at the roadside and set off up the track. As he came round a curve he experienced a mental jolt. Half-unconsciously he had carried in his mind from boyhood a picture of Anstey's Farm and its setting built up from some faded snapshots and his father's reminiscences. From the latter he had visualised a carefree life in almost unlimited space diversified by precipitous slopes, stretches of dense

10

woodland, a rushing torrent and a great mountain barrier at the head of the combe. All these features formed a backcloth for the large impressive house that was the family home. Now, confronted with reality, he had a claustrophobic feeling. The valley was narrow and shut in, the rushing torrent a small shallow stream and the mountain barrier merely the shoulder of Sinneldon. The house of his imagination had shrunk to a featureless rectangular building in a poor state of repair. Martin stood and stared and then grinned at his shattered illusions based on his father's idealised recollections.

The house was shuttered, and it was evident that no one was in residence, but he went through the formality of knocking and listening to the sound reverberating through the emptiness within. Either his uncle had not been down recently, and his own letter suggesting a visit was lying on the mat inside, or the proposed contact was not on. An attempt to peer through the slats of the shutters was unsuccessful. Going round to the back of the house Martin noted the limited amenities and the need for extensive repairs. Finally, after a last look at the front he began to retrace his steps, deep in thought. It had struck him that sooner or later he would be in for a problem. Possibly sooner. Paul was in his sixties, and on his demise he, Martin, would have this set-up round his neck. Living in it would be out of the question, of course. It was far too remote and needed a packet spending on it. Hardly saleable, unless some tycoon suddenly fell for the idea of the sort of simple life that only the really wealthy can afford. . . . But if the place was unsaleable, could one just leave it to fall down? What would the legal position be if somebody broke in and the roof collapsed on him?

As he arrived back at his car Martin was suddenly struck by another idea. Why not refuse the bequest? Surely there must be some legal way of doing this?

11

Obviously the thing to do was to get hold of a good solicitor. Somebody in the department at Randall's would be able to put him on to one. Having decided on this course of action he looked at his watch. It was a quarter to five. Over an hour to opening time, but he would go on to Dollaford, the nearest village to Anstey's Farm which his father had often talked about. As a kid he'd bought whacking great sweets called gobstoppers at the shop there for a ha'penny a time, and had said the place had a pretty decent pub. After a drink there perhaps the best thing would be to go back to Highcastle and put up somewhere for the night. Or possibly to go on to Polharbour. Still feeling a faint sense of disillusionment at the outcome of his trip up to date, Martin started up the Austin Maestro and eased it off the grass verge on to the road.

Traffic was light and he drove slowly, enjoying the fresh green of early summer and the wealth of wild flowers in the hedges. Presently a standardised development of small modern houses came in sight. Beyond this was the old-established village, a unplanned scatter of stone and cob cottages round a small grey church. Close to the latter was a house appreciably larger than its neighbours and standing back from the main road. It was solidly built of Crownmoor granite, two-storied and wreathed in wisteria. A board over the front door was inscribed THE PEATCUTTERS INN. 1664. Underneath the inscription was a boldly painted scene of two peatcutters in outmoded rustic garb armed with the long-handled tools of their trade, and in process of adding to a pile of neatly cut turves. The front door was massive and uncompromisingly shut. Over it an official notice stated that the proprietor of the inn was Maynard George Hooper, licensed to sell wines, spirits and beers on or off the premises.

Martin Anstey had got out of his car and was absorbing this information when the door suddenly opened. A girl appeared on the threshold and took a step forward. On catching sight of him she stopped and smiled.

'Anything we can do for you?' she asked. 'Short of opening up the bar before zero hour, that is.'

Martin registered a slight figure in blue and white separates, an oval face tapering to a delicate little chin, a mouth a shade big for beauty and lovely deep blue eyes. Soft brown hair was centrally parted and swept back. And the overall effect? A complete openness, a kind of inner luminosity . . . The phrase 'no darkness at all' suddenly flashed across his mind . . .

'Well,' he said, 'I suppose I'm a bit late for a cup of tea, aren't I?'

The girl glanced at her watch.

'We're supposed to stop laying on teas at five,' she told him, 'but let's stretch a point. I don't really belong here, so why worry? Could you just run your car round to the back? The road's a bit narrow here and there's a car park behind the pub, just up that lane at the side.'

Martin heard himself thanking her rather incoherently and leapt into the driving seat.

When he returned from the car park a few minutes later he found that the front door had been left open for him and he walked into a cool stone-flagged passage. The bar, still closed, was on the left. On the right a door with the notice DINING-ROOM was ajar. He pushed it open and found himself in a large room with about a dozen tables attractively laid for dinner, each with its vase of assorted sweet peas. About half the tables had RESERVED on them. It was obvious that the Peatcutters appealed to a wider public than merely the local drinkers of Dollaford. Near the door four tables were laid for tea, two of which had recently been in use. Martin heard footsteps and turned as they approached with a degree of anticipation that astonished him.

'Some tea will be along in just a few minutes,' she told him. 'Let's sit down. Part of an innkeeper's job is to make guests feel welcome and entertain them. Have you come far? I'm sure that's a standard opening gambit.'

'I drove down from London this morning,' he told her. 'Stopped off in Highcastle for an hour or two, and came on to call on an uncle who lives near here but drew a blank. I'd written to him to say I'd be turning up this afternoon but the house was shut up from the look of it. Not a sign of life, anyway. He probably hadn't had my letter. His place is a bit off the map, Anstey's Farm, it's called.'

He glanced up to find her looking at him in astonishment.

'Paul Anstey's your uncle?' she exclaimed. 'He blows in here for a drink or a meal when he's down from London, but I'm sure he's never mentioned a nephew living up there. Are you an Anstey too?'

'Yes. I'm Martin Anstey, his late younger brother's son. My family's been in Southern Rhodesia – Zimbabwe – since 1945. I was born there, and –'

A woman appeared in the doorway carrying a tray complete with teapot, milk and hot water jug, and a plate of scones and small cakes. Her straight grey hair was strained back off her face into a bun, and she wore old-fashioned gold-rimmed spectacles.

'Jo!' the girl exclaimed. 'What do you think? This gentleman's Martin Anstey – Paul Anstey's nephew. Martin, this is Jo Venner who helps us out.'

Ignoring Martin's greeting, the new arrival deposited the tray on the table and stared at him, tight-lipped.

'First I've heard of Paul Anstey having a nephew,' she said. 'Doesn't do to believe everything you're told,' she added as she made for the door.

14

'Situation defused! Not to worry – Jo's like that, but a tower of strength. You look a bit stunned. I'd better introduce myself, hadn't I? I'm Gemma Ford. Maynard Hooper who owns this pub is my uncle by marriage. I often pop down here for a few days when I've got some time off. My mother was Mrs Hooper's sister.'

Martin met her eyes which were full of laughter and fumbled for words.

'Well, I'm glad you were here today,' he heard himself say.

'What a nice thing to have said to one . . .. I think that's my uncle just coming in. Unk,' she called in the direction of the door.

A man appeared on the threshold, a tall, well-built and confident figure. His deep-set grey eyes surveyed the pair at the teatable.

'Hello! Which of your boy-friends is this one, Gemma?'

'None of them, Unk. You won't believe it, but this is Martin Anstey, Paul Anstey's nephew. And he lives in London, too!'

The information evoked an expression of astonishment verging on incredulity on Maynard Hooper's rather impassive face.

'Well, I'm damned,' he said. 'May I join you? Paul Anstey's been dropping in here at intervals ever since I bought the place eight years ago, and your existence has never been mentioned, although my wife and I know him as well as anyone does round here. Not that it adds up to very much. He only comes down for odd weekends and an occasional day or two. He was around last weekend, actually. One wonders why he keeps the place on. Do you see much of him in Town?'

'I only fetched up there myself a few months ago,' Martin replied, 'and up to now I've never set eyes on him.

Perhaps it would make more sense if I filled you in with a spot of our family history.'

He embarked on a much-condensed account of the Ansteys from the acquisition of the farm in the mid-nineteenth century to the present moment, playing down the relations between his grandfather, his uncle and his own father, and filling it out with his own life in Zimbabwe and South Africa. When it came to an end he got a shrewd glance from Maynard Hooper.

'So on returning to the Old Country you decided to have a bash at establishing your only known family link?'

'Frankly I couldn't care less about the family link,' Martin told him. 'I'm only trying to get in touch with Uncle Paul in order to check up on my position under my grandfather's Will. You see, Paul was only left a life interest in Anstey's Farm. If he died without a legitimate heir it was to revert to my father and ultimately to myself, being his eldest son.'

Maynard Hooper's eyebrows went up. He contemplated Martin with interest.

'Assuming that Paul Anstey hasn't produced a legitimate heir, what's your reaction to your ultimate inheritance, if I may ask?'

Martin grinned.

'Having made the journey down here and seen the place and the state it's been allowed to get into, my reaction is to get on to the lawyers and see if it's possible to refuse the reversion. I don't want a dump like that on my back.'

'You know, all this really is damned interesting,' Maynard Hooper said. 'It's starting to ring a few bells, too. Of course old John Anstey was before our time, but he was still a talking point to some extent in my early days here. Apparently he insisted on living out there entirely on his own. Then one day the poor old bastard was found dead in

16

his bed. The PM verdict was death from heart failure. It must have been quite sudden: he was only seventy, and fit for his age. Paul must have been out of touch for years. It wasn't until after the funeral that the solicitors managed to run him to earth. The village was outraged: funerals are taken seriously in these parts. But I don't seem to remember any mention of another son. Your visit will be the Dollaford sensation of the year.'

'Where are you going on to from here?' Gemma asked casually.

'I haven't really got on to planning my next move.' Martin made an effort to sound equally casual. 'I suppose I had a subconscious idea that I might get put up for the night by Uncle Paul. Perhaps I'd better push on to Polharbour.'

'For heaven's sake don't. It's simply ghastly at this time of year, isn't it, Unk?'

'Bloody is an understatement. Packed out with semi-nudes licking ice-cream and guzzling crisps. Blaring transistors and huge bulging women in bikinis. Why not stay the night here? We've got a couple of bedrooms, and as far as I know, the single's still vacant, isn't it Gemma?'

'Yes,' she replied. 'Only the double's been booked so far. A couple rang in from Highcastle.'

'Well, this seems a pretty good idea,' Martin said. 'Thanks, I'd like to say overnight.'

'We can feed you, of course,' Maynard Hooper told him. 'We lay on a specially good dinner at weekends. Put a "reserved" card on one of the single tables, Gemma.' He glanced at his watch. 'I'd better open up. It sounds like a chap with a thirst hovering in the passage. Come and have one on the house before you eat,' he invited Martin. 'Gemma'll show you your room and whatever. Sorry my wife's away this weekend. She'd have been interested to meet you.'

17

As he went out of the dining-room Gemma began to stack the tea things on a tray.

'I'll just get these along to the kitchen,' she said, 'and then take you on an escorted tour of the upper regions.' As she spoke a woman in a white overall appeared in the doorway: 'Sorry tea's gone on a bit late, Jo, but we've had such a surprise. This gentleman really does turn out to be a nephew of Paul Anstey. He blew in by chance and is staying overnight. Mr Martin Anstey . . . As I told you, this is Miss Jo Venner, the prop and mainstay of the Peatcutters. She lives in the cottage just across the lane up to the car park.'

Martin again greeted the grey-haired woman with a close-lipped capable face. He received a sharp look and the briefest of acknowledgements as she collected the tray and went out again.

'Not what you'd call a conversationalist, but so competent it isn't true,' Gemma said. 'Come along up and see where we're putting you, and then you can go and collect your gear and bring it in.'

The small bedroom was simple and attractive. Dead right for a place like this, he thought.

'This is it,' Gemma replied in answer to his comments after she had shown him round. 'Uncle Maynard's simply transformed this pub. It was all fusty and gone to seed when he bought it. It's his thing, revitalising fossilised pubs and small hotels. Then when the job's done he gets bored, sells the place as a going concern and moves on. I suspect he's beginning to get itchy feet here, as it's impossible to build on to the place as he'd like to and he thinks the tourist potential round here is enormous. . . . Well, I'll leave you to it. The bar's just opposite the dining-room.'

Martin, only half-listening as he struggled to find the words he wanted, hurriedly detained her.

18

'I say, look here, I don't want to spend the evening in a bar fug talking about my grandfather. What about a stroll later? Or a drive somewhere if you'd rather?'

Gemma paused, her hand on the door knob. Their eyes met briefly.

'All right,' she said. 'I'll rescue you somehow after a bit.'

When the door closed behind her Martin sat down on the edge of the bed and tried to assemble his thoughts coherently. Meeting with little success he went downstairs to collect his belongings from the car park. On returning he discerned notes of incredulity in the babble emanating from the bar. Later, fortified by a bath and a clean shirt, he made his entry to a sudden hush and the realisation that every face in the room was turned in his direction.

As he drank the one on the house pressed on him by Maynard Hooper and his share in a round tentatively proposed by himself, a flood of reminiscences and questions broke out. It was noticeable, Martin thought, that Paul Anstey was hardly mentioned in spite of the fact that he now occupied the family home. To his surprise and pleasure his father was clearly remembered by one or two of the older men, including a farmer for whom Hugh Anstey had worked before joining up in 1939. There were many questions about life in Zimbabwe, and why Martin had decided to come back and what his present job was. Finally, urged by Maynard Hooper to go and eat, he managed to extricate himself and headed for the dining-room. Here he enjoyed a good and very competently served meal. Two couples at the next table were friendly, and at the end of dinner he accepted their invitation to join them in the bar. Better than further cross-examination by the locals, he thought, wondering how long it would be before Gemma rescued him. By now the

19

bar was crowded and rather noisy. On one occasion he was conscious of being scrutinised and looked up just in time to catch a further keen look from the dour woman who had brought the tea tray, and who was now behind an open hatch apparently connecting the bar with the kitchen. Then, at long last and unheralded, Gemma was beside him, skilfully conveying that he was wanted. With apologies to his companions he followed her out into the passage. Before they both laughed, an exchange of glances as swift as thought acknowledged that the manoeuvre had been a matter of importance.

'Neatly done,' Martin told her. 'Where do we go from here?'

'If you feel you can face any more driving today there's a very steep minor road which would take us up Sinneldon in ten minutes. It's cooler there, and a super sunset's building up. I can't wait to hear all about South Africa and Rhodesia.'

'Fine,' he said, correctly diagnosing a warning impersonal note, 'Meet you at the car in five minutes.'

The minor road turned out to be a steep grass-grown track which gained height by a series of hairpin bends and petered out near the crest of Sinneldon.

'Of course I wouldn't have suggested coming up this way to everybody,' Gemma remarked as Martin drew up and switched off the engine, 'but of course you'll have had plenty of non-motorway experience in Africa. But you won't have had many sunsets to beat this one.'

'I'll grant you that,' he said.

The panorama of fields and woods which had fascinated the Pollards was now absorbed into the creeping dusk. Its former colours now intensified, the dying sun illuminated the north-western horizon in a flamboyant display of crimson, gold and primrose yellow. Overhead the vault of the sky was a pale luminous green, soon to be pierced by stars.

Gemma, curled at a discreet distance in the passenger seat, suddenly broke the silence.

'I'm not madly keen on your Uncle Paul,' she observed.

'What sort of a bloke is he?' Martin asked.

'Too right, somehow, and definitely patronising. You know the type. Well-preserved and dressed like a photograph in a glossy of a successful business man dropping in on his local. Cagey about his interests except in the most general terms. You know, my guess is that he did get your letter saying you were coming down and decided to opt out.'

'Mine too,' Martin agreed. 'As far as I gathered from my father he opted out completely from about 1934, when my grandfather couldn't afford Oxbridge for him and got him a job in London instead. I can't believe he'd welcome my turning up out of the blue like this. I said in my letter that I'd got a job but he'd probably think I wanted to cadge.'

'I say,' Gemma said after a pause. 'You'll get hold of a good solicitor over this Anstey's Farm business, won't you?'

The implication of concern for his own welfare behind this query was like the experience of a mild electric shock.

'You bet,' he replied. 'Your turn now to produce a *curriculum vitae*.'

'Tame after yours. The only child of rather elderly parents, boarding school, Oxford, English degree and at present a job I like immensely, buying books for the children's section of a group of London libraries.'

'Does the UK feel claustrophobic after the great open spaces,' she asked after another pause.

'Not geographically, certainly: "*Infinite riches in a little room*". And certainly not psychologically.'

'You mean racism, apartheid and all that?'

21

'This is it.'

They talked on intermittently, feeling their way into each other's minds as the sunset's splendour waned.

'I don't suppose,' Martin said, suddenly transposing into a different key, 'that this is the first time you've been out in a chap's car after dinner? I've done this sort of thing myself, come to that.'

'No,' Gemma said, turning away her head and looking out of the window. 'It's not the first time.'

'But somehow different, isn't it?'

'Yes. Incredibly. We only met about five hours ago.'

'It looks rather as though an exchange of telephone numbers is called for, don't you think?'

She faced him in the half-light and put out her hand.

'Yes it does. But it's – well – too important to hurry.'

'Far too important,' he agreed, taking her hand and drawing her towards him. 'One kiss, though, and we'll symbolically hazard our lives together by negotiating this precipice in the dark.'

An early start for London on the following morning was inescapable for Martin. Regrettably Gemma had her own car and would be driving up later. Short of sudden total disablement a newly-joined member of Randall's did not renege on his first invitation to dine at the Director's private residence. Martin was seen off by Maynard Hooper and Gemma who stood waving farewell at the door of the Peatcutters. They vanished abruptly from the driving mirror together with the inn itself as the car rounded a curve in the village street. For a split second the past twenty-four hours seemed to vanish with them. Then the indisputable existence of two entries in Martin's pocket diary restored their credibility: Gemma's telephone number and a dinner date with her on Sunday evening.

He had a good visual memory for roads and soon saw that he was almost at the bridge and track leading to Anstey's Farm. In the same moment he decided on impulse to pay the latter a second visit. It was conceivable that Paul Anstey had come down late on the previous night. Anyway, if he went up to the house again it couldn't be said that he, Martin, hadn't tried to make contact. He slowed down, parked at the roadside almost in the same place as before and set off on foot. There was more cloud today. The combe and the slopes of Sinneldon looked forbidding, he thought, and the house ever more down at heel. He went through the ritual of knocking twice and once again made a cursory inspection of the back premises. There was absolutely no sign of life. He had just returned to the front of the building when he heard a car on the road slow down. . . . A bit traumatic if they were going to meet on the doorstep. . . . He took a few steps forward and waited. After a couple of moments, however, the car drove on.

Five minutes later Martin himself was heading for London by way of Highcastle.

Chapter 3

Henry Watts, a brisk little man in his late fifties, was
storekeeper to a Highcastle building firm, carrying out his
duties competently from Monday to Friday. Saturdays
were allotted to his home for any necessary repairs or
redecorating, gardening, and the weekly expedition to
the supermarket with his wife. In view of all this steadfast
devotion to duty he felt justified in reserving alternate
Sundays for his hobby: he was an enthusiastic
birdwatcher.

On the day following the return to London of the
Pollards and Martin Anstey he made an early start,
getting a lift from a friend who delivered the Sunday
papers to the villages in the Sinnel valley. A reliable
report of sightings of buzzards in the Sinneldon area of
Crownmoor was drawing him there like a powerful mag-
net. He parted from his friend at Dollaford and went up
Sinneldon by the steep track used by Martin Anstey and
Gemma Ford on the previous Friday evening. He had
already decided to make for Grouch Tor, knowing that
rabbits were successfully re-establishing themselves
there.

He made his way purposefully along the track which
the Pollards had followed earlier, businesslike in his

summer birdwatching outfit of old grey trousers and blue cotton shirt. In his rucksack he carried notebook, small first-aid outfit and a packed lunch, and was equipped with first-rate binoculars and camera with a telescopic lens, bought with an unexpectedly handsome Ernie win. He paused at intervals to record some sightings of minor importance, keeping a watchful eye on the skies over-head. The Grouch Tor area was disappointing, and he pressed on, to stop suddenly on seeing dark specks in the blue expanse above. He had just arrived at the dwarf hawthorns and abandoned fields close to the head of the combe leading down to Anstey's Farm and quickly found what cover he could. As he watched, the dark specks evolved unmistakably into a couple of pairs of buzzards circling overhead in descending and diminishing spirals with their great wings characteristically upcurved at the tips. Abruptly one bird dropped out of the sky on to prey sighted on the ground. Henry Watts held his breath. Never before had he been in at the death like this, getting so close a view of the rich brown plumage, the speckled breast and cruel predatory beak. His hand trembled as he focused his camera. Suddenly the even larger female bird alighted to share the kill. From overhead came the melan-choly whistling of the second pair of buzzards circling hopefully. Finally, the victim disposed of, the successful predator and his mate took off with a short rush and soared upwards once more.

Henry Watts, aching from the effort of remaining motionless, relaxed, and emerged from the prickly haw-thorns. He sat down on the heather and began to make notes with feverish intensity. He was so absorbed that several minutes passed before he became half-consciously aware of something disturbing. The next moment he sprang to his feet, alerted by the unmistakable smell of burning. As he surveyed the wide sweep of the

25

moor a light breeze coming from the south-east brought acrid smoke which made him cough. Realising that it must be coming up the combe he hastily seized his belongings and ran to the beginning of the rough path down through the trees, memories of scorched and blackened tracks of Crownmoor left by previous heath fires vivid in his mind. He went down the steep stony path through the trees in the upper part of the combe at reckless speed, steadying himself by clutching at over-hanging branches and the slender trunks of saplings. The smoke became denser but to his relief there was so far no sound of the roaring and crackling of a heath fire out of control. At last he was clear of the trees and stopped dead in his tracks. The smoke was not coming from burning heather and bracken but from the partly collapsed farmhouse which he remember from a previous visit to the combe. About a third of the roof had fallen in and blue coils were wreathing slowly upwards and snaking from the gaping rectangles of the former windows. The nearer end of the house was still standing. There was no sign of life.

Henry Watts was a practical man used to responsibility. He summed up the situation in a few seconds. For some reason the flames had not spread through the whole house, but the fire was obviously smouldering, and it only needed the wind to get up a bit and there would be a blaze which would finish the job and set alight the dry grass and shrubs around. Too dangerous to go inside to see if any survivors were in the rooms still standing. Anybody asleep there would have been suffocated by the smoke, anyway. The urgent job was to get a fire brigade along before things could get out of hand.

He hurried down the track to the road as fast as he dared. No sense in dropping down dead with a coronary: he wasn't as young as he was. Rounding the bend at the bottom of the combe he saw a car flash past and thought hopefully that the fine Sunday would be bringing folk out on the roads. He crossed the bridge and shook his fist at an old Morris packed with teenagers who yelled at his frantic signals and shot by. The next car was an impeccably maintained Cortina which contained an elderly couple. The driver hesitated, torn between suspicion and a sense of moral responsibility towards a respectable-looking citizen apparently in trouble. He drew up. Henry Watts ran to the driver's window.

'For God's sake get me to a phone quick,' he said breathlessly. 'There's a farmhouse on fire up that combe.'

Within ten minutes he was dialling 999 for the first time in his life and reporting FIRE . . . He was through, and giving the chap at the other end the facts. . . . He was being told to wait at the kiosk to be picked up and show them the way . . .

As he waited a gratifying sense of having kept his head crept over him, followed by an exciting realisation that he might be mentioned in the next day's issue of the *Highcastle Evening News . . .*

Within half an hour there was an invasion of the combe on a scale unseen since the palmy days of the late nine-teenth century when meets of the Crownmoor Hunt took place on occasions at Anstey's Farm. Henry Watts, instructed to wait as he might be required to make a statement, watched the purposeful deployment of firemen with interest. The County Fire Service, only too well acquainted with the potential hazards of heath fires especially after a spell of dry weather, had sent out three fire engines with their water tenders. The nearest, from the little town of Leeford, arrived first with its Station Officer, and was followed in a surprisingly short space of time by more powerful engines from Polharbour and Highcastle. Close behind came an ambulance and a

27

police car bringing Detective-Inspector Parkin of the County CID and a constable driver from Highcastle. Powerful jets of water were played on the smouldering ruins, while firemen with breathing apparatus penetrated the relatively intact section of the house. Meanwhile a wide area round the building was being systematically damped down, and a watch kept on trees and shrubs in the upper part of the combe. After a time firemen emerged from the surviving rooms and reported to the Assistant Divisional Officer who had come out with the Highcastle brigade. It seemed obvious, Henry Watts thought, that at least no victims overcome by smoke fumes had been found. His reflections were interrupted by the constable bringing a message that Detective-Inspector Parkin would like a word with him in the police car.

The two men had met before in connection with a break-in at the building firm for which Henry Watts worked.

'Bit off your normal beat, isn't it?' Inspector Parkin asked when they had exchanged greetings.

'I was birdwatching up on Sinneldon,' Henry Watts told him, 'and got within yards of a pair of buzzards who put paid to a rabbit or maybe a mole. You don't get all that many buzzards on Crownmoor these days.'

'I wouldn't know a buzzard from a blackbird myself,' Inspector Parkin declared. 'The thing is, can you remember when you first spotted smoke coming up from here? Constable Trott'll jot down a few points for our report.'

Henry Watts gave his name, age, address and place of work, and after some calculation thought he had first noticed the smoke around half-past one.

'I smelt it first,' he said, 'but couldn't seé a sign of it up top. So I reckoned it must be coming from here, and scrambled down that path at the head of the combe. It soon got denser, and as I came clear of the trees I saw that'

28

– he indicated the remains of Anstey's Farm. 'I belted down to the footbridge, and saw the place was still smouldering and could flare up any moment if the wind picked up, and start a big heath fire with everything dry as a chip after this drought. There was nothing I could do on the spot, so I made for the road and hitched a lift to the Dollaford call box. There wasn't a sign of anybody about at the farm,' he added.

'What you did was dead right. Pity everybody doesn't keep their head like that in an emergency. . . . Yes, what is it?'

A fireman had appeared at the window of the police car.

'The Assistant Divisional Officer would like a word with you, sir,' he told Parkin.

'OK. Hang on, Mr Watts, will you?'

While Constable Trott made a fair copy of his notes, Henry Watts watched Inspector Parkin peering through the empty window spaces of the burnt-out part of the farm, and conferring with the Assistant Divisional Officer and the Station Officers from Polharbour and Leeford. After a time the group disappeared round the back of the building.

'Hope they haven't found what's left of some poor bastard in there,' he commented presently.

'Might well have,' Constable Trott agreed as the four men reappeared and stood deep in discussion for some minutes. Finally Inspector Parkin detached himself and came back to the police car, his face impassive.

'We needn't hold you up any longer, Mr Watts,' he said. 'Trott will run you over to Leeford and you'll be able to pick up a bus back to Highcastle from there. You've given us some useful information. Thanks a lot.'

He went off again briskly, a fair-haired man in his early forties with observant blue eyes and a preoccupied

29

expression on his face. Henry Watts was grateful for the lift after an unexpectedly demanding day, and was now being consumed with the desire to get home and regale his family and friends with an account of his experiences. On the road he agreed with Constable Trott that they'd spotted a stiff in the wreckage for sure.

What, in fact, had been discovered by the fireman was not a charred body but unmistakable signs of arson. The shed serving as a paraffin store had been broken into and a quantity of paraffin poured into the house through a smashed window at the back, the slats of the latter's protective shutter having been partly wrenched away. A single lighted match would have been adequate to start off an explosive flare-up. The pungent smell of paraffin was still strong.

Inspector Parkin expressed his views on vandals in robust terms while experiencing a sense of satisfaction. A tidy-minded man, he liked straightforward cases that could be cleared up with no loose ends. There had been something decidedly off-key about an unoccupied house at the back-of-beyond suddenly going on fire for no apparent reason. He was also, however, a well-trained and highly conscientious officer, and stood for a few moments casting about in his mind for any unusual aspects of the situation.

'A bit rum that the whole house didn't go up, wasn't it?' he asked the Highcastle Assistant Divisional Fire Officer.

'Not all that rum now that we can see that the place was built in stages. It began as a pretty primitive long-house. Just a shippon where the kitchen is, separated by a cross-passage – the present hall – from the fair-sized room where the people lived. Another ground floor room was added later but a hefty great outer wall of granite blocks separated it from the first room, if you get me. It was this wall which helped to confine and slow down the fire which the arson bloke started in the room at the far end.'

'Interesting,' Parkin commented. 'What about the upper storey?'

'That was added much later and is all of a piece, and the fire spread along further than downstairs, and eventually part of the roof caved in. But the outside walls were granite and the oak beams hard as iron which again slowed things down. Added to which, there wasn't a breath of wind last night, and every window was shut. Most of what furniture there was seems to have been big old-fashioned heavy stuff. It all adds up, you see.'

Parkin nodded.

'Thanks,' he said. 'That's made things much clearer. About timing, now. The chap who raised the alarm says he first smelt smoke about half-past one when he was birdwatching up on Sinneldon. He belted down into the combe and says the house was in much the same state as when you people got here. Does this give you any idea of what time the fire could have started?'

'Not within an hour or two', the expert replied, 'bearing in mind the special conditions I've been talking about. But it must have been light enough for the fire-raiser to find the paraffin store, burst it open and smash the shutter of the back window in that end room. Say three to four o'clock. Not earlier I'd say, judging from the damage done this morning. Just about the time when a bunch of thugs could've been coming away from an all-night booze and drugs binge.'

'Shouldn't be difficult to get on the track of a gang like that,' Parkin replied. The enquiry into the fire, he reflected, was getting off to a satisfactory start. The next job was to find out who owned the dump. At the sound of a car coming up from the road he turned in some surprise: Constable Trott could hardly have done the Leeford trip in the time. It was not, however, the police car but a

Volvo, and a man had got out and was helping a grey-haired woman passenger to extricate herself. As Parkin went forward intending to challenge them, the man, tall and with an assured air, came to meet him.

'I'm Hooper, landlord of the Peatcutters at Dollaford, Inspector,' he said. 'The news of this business has got to the village and I thought I'd better run over in case I could provide any information you want. The owner of the house only comes down for odd weekends. This lady here is Miss Venner of Dollaford who works for him: Mr Paul Anstey, a London businessman, and she lends a hand at the Peatcutters, too.'

Parkin greeted her pleasantly but she was unresponsive.

'I'm grateful to you for coming along, sir,' he said to Maynard Hooper. 'Saves me a trip to Dollaford. I've had to send the police car over to Leeford, so perhaps I could join you and Miss Venner in yours for a few minutes when I've just got things taped with the Fire Service people?'

'Of course. We'll go and wait in it.'

The firemen were already collecting up their gear. After consultation between the officers and Parkin it was settled that the brigades should leave, two men remaining overnight as a precautionary measure. Reliefs for the two left on duty would be sent out from the headquarters at Highcastle. As the various fire appliances began to leave, Parkin went over to join Maynard Hooper and Miss Venner who were sitting in the former's car. He took the passenger seat beside Hooper who was smoking a cigarette at the wheel and half turned to get a good view of Miss Venner in the back seat. Somewhere in her sixties, he thought, noting a determined chin and a guarded expression in the grey eyes behind her spectacles. On the defensive, he thought, and wondered if she was afraid of being held responsible for the fire through some carelessness while working at the farm. It struck him that she was well turned out for her station: natty summer outfit with matching accessories, but these days competent domestic labour was a paying proposition. He turned his attention to the landlord of the up-and-coming Peatcutters Inn at Dollaford.

He was soon in possession of the facts of Paul Anstey's intermittent appearances for drinks and odd meals at the pub when in residence at Anstey's Farm. The most recent one had been a week ago when he had come down for the weekend.

'Of course I can't swear that he hasn't been down for a night or two since,' Hooper added, 'but he didn't turn up at our place. And he must have pushed off again early on Friday at latest.'

'Why?' Parkin asked.

'Because his nephew, Martin Anstey, had written to him at the farm to say he'd look in sometime on the Friday afternoon. This last Friday afternoon. He found the place all shut up and got no answer when he banged on the door.'

'Did this Mr Martin Anstey come on to the Peatcutters, then?'

'That's right. He stayed overnight and went back to London early yesterday morning.'

Parkin considered.

'Well, we must get on to Mr Paul Anstey at once, of course, and report the fire and the extent of the damage. You'll have his address, I take it, Miss Venner, as you work for him?'

'*Going Places*, 170 Wendover Row, London W1', she replied reluctantly.

Parkin stared at her.,

'What did you say? *Going Places*?'

'Anstey runs a travel firm,' Maynard Hooper interposed.'

'Well, that's his business address, I take it? That's no use on a Sunday. It's his private address we need, Miss Venner.'

'I don't know nothing about that. When he's coming down he calls me on the phone. He had it put in and pays the rental. He doesn't write. I know his business address because it's on the brochures he leaves lying around at the farm.'

Parkin turned to Hooper.

'You'll have the nephew's address if he stayed at your pub on Friday night? I'll try getting on to Paul Anstey through him.'

'Martin Anstey's address is in our register all right, but I can tell you here and now that it won't be any use to you. They've never met. This is the situation . . .'

Stubbing out his cigarette he embarked on a condensed history of the Ansteys and the position in regard to the present and future ownership of the farm.

Parkin listened with growing annoyance. What had seemed a run-of-the-mill case of arson by a bunch of hooligans was beginning to develop time-consuming complications. He glanced round at the sound of a car coming up from the road, saw Constable Trott returning from Leeford and thought rapidly.

'Seeing that Mr Martin Anstey's legally involved in the ownership of this place he's entitled to be notified about what's happened. I'll follow on to Dollaford with you, sir, and get his address if you'll kindly let me have it, and we'll get on to Mr Paul Anstey as soon as his office opens tomorrow morning. It'll be urgent for the two of them to get together over the insurance and decide whether to rebuild and so forth.'

'I bet the insurance cover's minimal,' Hooper replied. 'Probably never been raised since old John Anstey's time, and nowhere near enough to cover current

34

rebuilding costs.'

'Still there's site value, for what it's worth,' Parkin replied as he got out of the car. 'Maybe a bit of land goes with the place, too. Well, sir, if you'll lead the way I'll follow on with my chap. Good evening, Miss Venner. Sorry if this means your job folding.'

He got no reply.

On his return to police headquarters at Highcastle with the keys of Anstey's farm extracted, Parkin's first action was to get out an urgent enquiry into any sightings of potential troublemakers in the area, between Saturday evening and roughly eight o'clock on Sunday morning, in connection with a serious case of arson at Anstey's Farm, between Affacombe and Dollaford. This done he dialled Martin Anstey's number but got only the ringing tone. In the course of writing a report on the incident for his Super he made a further unsuccessful attempt. He followed this up with a call to his wife telling her to expect him when she saw him. At his sixth attempt at eleven o'clock he got through. A masculine voice, which he identified as U but sounding a shade different somehow, repeated the number.

'Mr Martin Anstey?' he enquired.

'Speaking. Who's calling?'

'Inspector Parkin from Highcastle police headquarters, sir. I'm sorry to tell you that Anstey's Farm, near Dollaford, was badly damaged by fire during last night.'

He heard an incredulous exclamation.

'Good Lord!' Martin Anstey struggled to dispel the sense of floating on roseate clouds. He had proposed to Gemma over dinner and she had accepted him, even though expressing doubts about their joint sanity. 'What on earth can have happened?' he went on hastily. 'It was perfectly OK about ten yesterday morning when I went along on my way back here to see if my uncle, Mr Paul

Anstey, had turned up. Was the place struck by lightning or something?'

'No, sir. The fire was caused by deliberate arson. There's no doubt whatever about this.'

'But who on earth? Vandals cruising round full of booze, I suppose? I say, my uncle wasn't there, was he?'

'No. The Fire Service are satisfied that nobody was in the house. I've called you because we're anxious to get on to him at once as the owner. The woman from Dollaford who works for him had only got his business address.'

'Sorry, Inspector, but I can't help you. I was born and brought up in Southern Rhodesia, and have only been over here since March. He and my father, who died recently, were out of touch.'

'Was Mr Paul Anstey expecting you to visit him at the farm this weekend?'

'Well, I wrote to him there about ten days ago saying I'd look in on chance last Friday afternoon but he didn't answer, and the place was shut up when I got there. So I put up at the Dollaford pub for Friday night, had another bash on Saturday morning on impulse, and drew a blank again, and came back here. I got in just after four. The chap who rents the garage next to mine was just coming out. Davidson's his name.'

'We'll have to leave it overnight then,' Parkin said thankfully. 'I'll just give you Mr Paul Anstey's business address as you'll be wanting to contact him yourself, and you might let me know yours in case we need to contact you during the day.'

Jim Eastlake and Bob Forches, the two firemen who had volunteered for overnight standby duty at Anstey's Farm arrived by Fire Service car at about half-past eight. They unloaded thermos flasks of hot coffee, food supplies and miscellaneous equipment to make their vigil as comfortable as possible. A two-way radio had been provided to link them with the Fire Brigade headquarters if necessary.

'Brought everything but the kitchen sink from the looks of it,' remarked one of the departing pair. ' 'Ave a good night.'

'One of us got to stay awake, anyway, worse luck,' Bob Forches replied. 'Boss said the police patrol car'd be droppin' in. So long, then.'

The car bumped off down the track and disappeared. The new arrivals installed themselves on the grassy terrace in front of the surviving section of the farm, and settled down to enjoy a cup of coffee and a smoke. They watched the north-western sky gradually fade and deep shadow stealthily take possession of the combe. A surprising number of unexplained noises became audible: rustlings, grunts, chirps and flutters. A sudden strident 'tu-whit' from close at hand made Jim Eastlake start and swear.

'What the bloody 'ell's that?' he demanded as a large flying object glided soundlessly past them.

'Owl, you great chump. Never heard one before?'

'Not just be'ind my bloody shoulder, I 'aven't.'

They became acclimatised to their unfamiliar surroundings and the night passed peacefully enough. The police patrol put in an appearance soon after three o'clock, were told that there was nothing to report, accepted cups of coffee and drove off again. The firemen settled down once more, and presently occasional grunts indicated that Jim Eastlake had dropped off. Feeling bored, as the first faint glimmer of a new day appeared in the eastern sky, Bob Forches got up quietly, and went down to the little footbridge to watch the morning come up over the steep wall of the combe.

As the sky brightened moment by moment, his heart

gave a thump at the sudden appearance of a man's figure high above him, standing out clearly against the dawn and apparently looking down on the farm. More startling still the figure began to dance . . . leaping up and down . . . flinging arms and legs in the air and waving a handkerchief. Swift as thought, arsonists and lunatics linked up in Bob's mind. Cupping his mouth with his hands he shouted a challenge. The figure vanished with the speed of thought and Jim Eastlake came running . . .

They agreed that it was no good going up to try and catch the chap. He'd be half across Crownmoor by the time they got to the top, and anyway they couldn't leave their post. Maybe they'd got the answer, though. Somebody escaped from a loony bin who'd fired the place the night before and come back to have a look. They'd better put in a report, though, soon as they got back.

Chapter 4

On Monday morning Inspector Parkin arrived at his desk rather before his usual time. He was anxious to get all matters arising from the fire at Anstey's Farm dealt with as quickly as possible. There were other important cases on hand and he was due at the regular weekly conference with his Super and other senior police officers at eleven. His first step was to ring the telephone switchboard operator and ask for the number of a London travel agency called *Going Places* to be checked as quickly as possible. While he waited for this information he went through a small heap of reports on potential troublemakers who had been on the loose in the area on Saturday night. They were disappointingly negative, and none of them could be linked with the arson at the farm. The telephone number of *Going Places* was forthcoming, but he decided to wait until nine o'clock before making the call. No go, he thought, until there's somebody senior enough to be able to pass on Anstey's private number if he isn't there himself. He had just started to read his letters when the station's telephone operator called him again.

'Switchboard, sir. As the officer in charge of the enquiry into the fire at Anstey's Farm, Dollaford, will you accept a call from Detective-Chief Superintendent Pollard of New Scotland Yard?'

'Put him through,' Parkin managed to reply in what he hoped was a normal voice.

'Detective-Inspector Parkin of Highcastle? This is Detective-Chief Superintendent Tom Pollard speaking from the Yard. Am I right in taking it that you're handling the enquiry into a fire at Anstey's Farm on Saturday night, and that it's now accepted as a case of arson?'

'That's right, sir,' Parkin managed to reply.

'You'll be wondering how the heck I come into it,' the assured but warm and friendly voice went on. 'I was on leave last week and my wife and I were staying with a friend at Affacombe, a Mrs Strode. Last Friday morning she drove us out on the road to Polharbour about 12 miles and dropped us to go up on Sinneldon and do the walk back. About half-past three we were coming down the path into the combe where Anstey's Farm is, and as we stopped to look across at the place we saw a youngish man walking up the track from the road. He was wearing a light suit, and had dark hair a bit on the long side. He had a good look at the farm and then went up to the door and knocked. Nothing happened. The place looked completely shut up. He went round the back, inspected the various sheds and then had another go at the front door, after which he went off towards the road again. A few minutes later we heard a car drive away . . . I say, Inspector, you probably know about this chap already, but I thought I'd better put in a report to be on the safe side.'

Inspector Parkin made an inarticulate noise in his throat in an effort to find suitable words. 'Actually the chap had come forward,' he said, 'but there was nothing like getting a statement confirmed. We're most grateful to you for ringing in, sir,' he went on. 'So far we haven't managed to get on to the owner of the place, a Mr Paul Anstey. The young man is his nephew, but it seems they've never met. Not what you'd call a straightforward set-up.'

'Far from it, I gathered, when we were down there,' Pollard replied. 'Well, the best of luck, Inspector. I'll be watching the papers. Good hunting.'

He rang off. Replacing his receiver, Parkin sat dazed for a few moments. Then, snatching it up again he demanded to be connected with *Going Places*.

Announcing himself as Inspector Parkin speaking from Highcastle Police Headquarters he asked to be put through to Mr Paul Anstey. A startled feminine voice requested him to hold the line. After what seemed to him a longish wait a click inaugurated a conversation with a Mr James Spencer, the Office Manager.

'Mr Anstey isn't available, Inspector, I'm afraid,' he was told. 'He's in the States in connection with plans for holidays over there for our next year's programme. You're speaking from Highcastle, I understand? There's nothing wrong with his house near there, I hope?'

'Unfortunately, it was badly damaged by fire during Saturday night,' Parkin replied, 'and we're anxious to get in touch with him as soon as possible. No one in the area knew his private telephone number and he's not in the directory, so we have been held up as your office was closed yesterday, of course. Can you put us in touch with him, wherever he is at the moment?'

'Well, not until he rings in, I'm afraid. He's on the move with no fixed address, and calls us every two or three days in case any decisions are needed here.'

'When did he last call?'

'On Friday morning. He was on the point of leaving New Orleans and going on to the Grand Canyon area and California.'

41

'It looks as though he may contact you today, then, or at any rate tomorrow. When he does, please tell him about the fire and ask him to ring us immediately. I'll give you the number: Highcastle code, then 763551. Got that? Good. Now, would you please let me have his private address and telephone number as we shall probably need it on his return.'

Mr Spencer hesitated perceptibly.

'Mr Anstey has definite views on preserving his privacy from the firm's clients and has an ex-directory number. He can always be contacted here in business hours except at weekends.'

'We're dealing with a police matter,' Parkin replied brusquely. 'The fire at Anstey's Farm was caused by arson and the investigation's a priority, so may I have that address and number, please?'

Mr Spencer gave an incredulous exclamation and complied, still with obvious reluctance.

'Thanks,' Parkin said, noting down an affluent sounding address in Knightsbridge. 'And to repeat, be sure to ring us at Highcastle immediately that you are in touch with Mr Anstey, won't you? Goodbye, Mr Spencer.'

He rang off and leant back in his chair for a few moments mentally reviewing the situation. Satisfied that nothing further could be done at the moment over notifying Paul Anstey of his loss he began to work through the morning's mail and overnight reports. His brow furrowed as he read one from the Chief Fire Officer's office. It informed him that two reliable firemen had spent the night on standby duty at Anstey's Farm: J. Eastlake and R. Forches. The night had been without incident until Fireman Forches had sighted a man on the northern lip of the combe and looking down at the farm at about four-thirty a.m. This man had begun to behave eccentrically, leaping and flinging his arms in the air. On being challenged by Fireman Forches he had instantly disappeared. It had been judged impracticable to go up and search for him, and nothing further had been seen of him. The usual steps would be taken in the course of the day to prevent unauthorised access to the damaged building, and to put up notices warning the public to keep clear.

Mental derangement and arson instantly linked themselves in Parkin's mind as they had in Fireman Forches's. With a sense of mounting exasperation he set in motion an enquiry into disturbed persons in the area, all of whose activities during the two previous nights now needed investigation. He then attacked the remaining paperwork on his desk, clearing it just in time for the weekly conference at eleven.

The agenda was predictable, down to the special emphasis on the usual increased vandalism of the current holiday season. Inspector Parkin was asked to report on the arson at Anstey's Farm, and the steps he had taken were voted adequate. A modest increase in foot patrols at Polharbour on Saturday evenings was agreed upon.

Over lunch in the canteen Parkin's account of Detective-Chief Superintendent Pollard's phone call was listened to with interest.

'No side whatever,' he replied in response to enquiries. 'No Lord God Almighty touch. Might have been any ordinary friendly chap in another force.'

The conversation turned to the Affacombe murder case brought to a successful conclusion by Pollard about sixteen years earlier.

'He's gone to the top since then all right,' one of the older men who remembered the case remarked. 'Doesn't seem to have turned his head, though, from what Parkin says.'

Shortly afterwards the group broke up. On returning to

43

his desk Parkin was confronted by a large manila envelope marked URGENT. He opened it to find a smaller cheap white envelope addressed in block capitals to Highcastle Police Station. It had a first class stamp and the Highcastle District postmark. The date was the current one: June 18. The letter could, therefore, have been posted at any time after the last postbox clearance on the morning of Saturday, 16 June, probably in Highcastle itself as it had arrived by the second delivery on Monday. Reflecting ironically that this had been smart work on the part of the GPO, Parkin examined the envelope carefully. He saw that it had already been treated for dabs. Inside he found a similarly treated single sheet of cheap white writing paper with a message in the same block capitals.

'What about that posh dark blue Austin Maestro parked on the side of the road where the track goes up to Anstey's Farm Saturday morning twenty-past ten car number OJ37 OFLZ with nobody in it. Head towards Highcastle, makes you think don't it?'

Parkin read the message several times and sat considering it. The car was obviously young Anstey's, he decided, left parked on the roadside while he went up for that second call at the farm. Right place and right time, assuming that the young chap had been speaking the truth. Still, there'd better be a check. He put in hand a telephone enquiry to the Greater London Vehicle Licensing Authority, and then made a call to the Peatcutters Inn. Maynard Hooper himself replied, and when asked about young Martin Anstey's car described it without hesitation as a dark blue Austin Maestro. He added that it was the most recent model and that he could have done with it himself. Parkin thanked him and rang off. Shortly afterwards the licensing authority confirmed the registration number as that of Martin Anstey.

44

Before filing the anonymous letter, Parkin read it once more. The note of malice stood out a mile, he thought. Somebody had got it in for young Anstey all right. Odd, when you came to think about it, seeing that he'd only been in the UK for a few months. Could it possibly have been sent by whoever started the fire as a means of getting somebody else suspected? The crazy dancing bloke seen by the fireman, for instance? In that case it was just a stroke of luck for the writer that a car happened to be parked at the beginning of the track just where he happened to drive past on the Saturday morning with his scheme for arson all lined up . . .

Finally, feeling that the fire was taking up too much of his time, Parkin filed the letter and turned his attention to other matters.

Early on Tuesday morning Mr Spencer of *Going Places* rang Highcastle to say that contact had been made with Paul Anstey. Mr Anstey was naturally upset on learning of the disaster to his family home, but felt that his business commitments in the States were too important to the firm for him to cancel them immediately. Any urgent matters arising from the fire could be dealt with by his Highcastle solicitors, Hepplewhite, Neale and Royland, who would inform his insurance company. Mr Anstey hoped to be back in London within the next fortnight.

On receiving this information Inspector Parkin promptly relegated the arson at Anstey's Farm to the background of his current preoccupations. It was not, however, destined to remain there for long.

Polharbour, which Maynard Hooper had described so luridly to Martin Anstey, had for centuries been a small fishing port. During the early twentieth century it had slowly evolved into a residential seaside town of modest

45

size. After World War Two a younger generation of its inhabitants began to realise its growth potential as a popular summer seaside resort and it had expanded explosively. Gift and antique shops, take-away food and snack bars and an amusement arcade had sprouted as if by magic. The narrow streets became impossibly crowded in the summer months and the traffic problem a nightmare to motorists. Enterprising descendants of the fishermen of the past invested in motor launches and brought in day trippers from other resorts along the coast. The two pubs, the Lobster Pot and the Admiral Benbow, bought up neighbouring properties, and both managed to increase their capacity, but they were packed out during opening hours. Minor disorders were frequent, and summer patrol duty at Polharbour was highly unpopular among the County police.

At about eight o'clock on the Tuesday evening of Paul Anstey's telephone conversation with Mr Spencer, a potentially ugly situation developed. A group of half a dozen leather-jacketed motor cyclists roared into the seafront area of the town. They were patently already the worse for drink, and both pubs refused them admission. Two shop windows were smashed, and the invaders charged through the narrow streets yelling obscenities and terrifying the crowds before leaving the town by the road to Highcastle.

All mobile police patrol vehicles in the area were alerted by radio and ordered to converge on the troublemakers. It was about eight miles out of Polharbour on the Highcastle road that the two men in one of the police cars sighted a man's body sprawled in the hedge. A brief inspection showed that he was severely injured and immediate radio contact was made with the ambulance station at Highcastle. On arrival the crew raised their eyebrows and radioed the casualty department at

46

Highcastle General Hospital as they started off with the injured man.

The Casualty Officer on duty was waiting in readiness and immediate steps were taken to establish the nature and extent of the man's injuries. He was wearing scruffy jeans and a dirty short waterproof coat. As this was being carefully removed a trickle of white powder came from inside it and ran down on the floor of the casualty department . . .

Several hours later when major surgery had been carried out and the patient transferred to the Intensive Care Unit, a small group conferred in one of the hospital's laboratories. It included the Casualty Officer, a forensic analyst, Superintendent Bainbridge and Inspector Parkin. Spread out before them on one of the benches were the man's clothing and the few contents of his rucksack. The white powder was found to be escaping from a torn waterproof packet in one of the inner pockets of the coat. It had now been officially identified as heroin. Similar but undamaged packets of the drug had been found in other inside pockets. A wallet contained fifty pounds in notes and some coins. There was no clue of any kind to the man's identity. But to the two police officers the most interesting finds were a key of the type supplied with a modern mortice lock and a dirty piece of paper with pencilled markings. These were difficult to make out at first, but highly magnified and put under strong lighting they resolved themselves into a rudimentary plan:

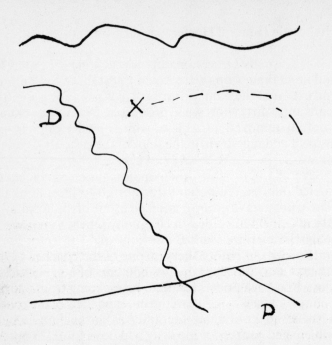

After some minutes of baffled contemplation, Inspector Parkin gave a sudden exclamation.

'It's that ruddy place cropping up again, sir. Anstey's Farm. How to get to it on foot from Polharbour. The stuff must have come in there and be going on to be dumped at the farm . . .'

Within the next hour the key had been tried and found to fit the farm's back door. Meanwhile the injured man died without regaining consciousness.

Chapter 5

By nine o'clock a top-level conference was in session at Highcastle police station.

'I've been on to the Drugs Department at the Yard,' the Chief Constable reported. 'Their reaction is that at all costs this business mustn't be allowed to leak out at the moment. They agree that it's obvious that Paul Anstey's letting his place be used as a collecting point for drugs which are probably coming in by boat. He may be organising a fair-sized network. The farm's isolated, but it's his own home which makes his irregular but quite frequent visits to it unremarkable. And he's London-based which is ideal for passing on the stuff to pushers with a virtually unlimited market.'

There was a general murmur of assent.

'All the same,' the Super went on, 'the Drugs Department want us to round up more evidence. Find the stuff on the premises if possible. Anstey's been away over two weekends now and it seems reasonable to think that anyway one other consignment's been dumped in the meantime. The arson's in our favour up to a point. Whoever's deputising for Anstey will hope that any heroin on the premises went up in smoke. I posted a couple of chaps at the farm an hour ago in case anyone turns up and tries to nose around. Any searching we do ourselves mustn't be all that obvious to people masquerading as hikers, for instance. Any suggestions?'

'What about "interests of public safety"?' Inspector Parkin suggested rather tentatively, conscious of representing the most junior rank present. 'I mean giving out that it's vital to make the burnt-out part of the house safe in case people like holiday makers go poking around?'

'You could be on to something there, Parkin,' the CC allowed. 'Get hold of a lorry with the right sort of equipment, and a squad of workmen to go out there to start clearing up the mess and making the place safe. Warning notices must be put up, of course. Not that they're likely to keep the fool public out. Then while the work's going on you and Ferris have a good look round the rest of the place, saying you're investigating the arson. It'll be a mucky job, but I'd rather you did it on your own. A squad of chaps would be a bit too obvious. Take the key that was on the bloke who was killed.'

No one had any further suggestions to put forward and Parkin was told to go ahead. Having made the necessary arrangements with a Highcastle firm of builders he drove out to Anstey's Farm with Detective-Sergeant Ferris. They parked outside the front of the house and walked round to the back premises. Parkin produced a labelled key from an inner pocket and inserted it in the mortice lock of the back door. It turned easily.

'Bob's your uncle,' he remarked, and went in, followed by Ferris.

They found themselves in what appeared to have been a small scullery at one time but was now bare and dusty. It had a bare floor of stone flags. They went down on hands and knees and examined these carefully but there was no sign of any of them having been disturbed since they were first laid. From the floor they turned their attention to the

50

walls, sounding them carefully but to no purpose. A cupboard contained nothing but dust, cobwebs and crumbling plaster.

The arrangements for the house's water supply seemed to them both decidedly primitive. It was piped in from the well outside, and had to be pumped by hand to the scullery sink and what was probably a bathroom on the floor above through a further Emmet array of pipes. Arrangements for heating the water by means of Calor gas appeared to have been installed comparatively recently.

'Surely there must have been a link-up with a kitchen stove originally,' Parkin said, opening a door. 'Yes, here it is, boarded up. Paul Anstey must have wanted something simpler and quicker for his weekends.'

The kitchen proper was a much larger room with a window on to the combe. Ferris opened the shutters. There were signs of limited domestic use: a gas cooker with its cylinder of bottled fuel, some cooking utensils and a limited quantity of cutlery, china and stores in cupboards. As in the scullery there was a stone-flagged floor. They checked this carefully and were sounding the walls when a lorry could be heard chugging up the track from the main road. They broke off for Parkin to talk to the builders' foreman, and decided to have a break and their sandwiches before tackling the boarded-up kitchen stove. Half an hour later they stood contemplating the latter unenthusiastically.

'There's nothing for it,' Parkin said gloomily, staring at the closely fitting wooden partition which stretched up to the dusty mantelpiece. 'It looks as though it hasn't been shifted since the day it was put up, but we can't afford to take any chances.'

They had brought an assortment of tools and with some difficulty prised the partition free. Behind it was an

51

antiquated kitchen stove with its ovens and dampers under a thick and undisturbed layer of dust and the miscellaneous debris that had fallen from the chimney.

'Museum piece if ever there was one,' Ferris remarked. 'I suppose the Ansteys had skivvies to blacklead it and stoke in those days, the poor devils.'

With the help of their torches they investigated the musty ovens. The stove itself was full of crumpled paper which had never burnt through. With some difficulty they refixed the wooden boarding, and managed to pump up some ice-cold water and have a sketchy wash at the sink in the scullery. This done, Parkin looked at his watch.

'We'll vet the hall and the stairs,' he said, 'and then call it a day. I heard the builder's chaps going off just now.'

Standing at the front door he remained for a few moments surveying the narrow hall which originally had been the cross passage between the shippon and the family quarters. Presumably, when the Ansteys bought the farm some time in the 1850s, they had blocked the far end of the passage with an outer wall. This had been carried upwards to form part of the upper storey which they had superimposed on the original long-house. A staircase leading up to it was adjacent to the wall, rising to the first floor in three short stages of four steps each, separated by half-landings.

'OK,' Parkin said. 'You vet the floor, Ferris, and vet every blasted join in the flags. I'll tackle the stairs.'

It was a substantial staircase of dark oak, clearly a relic of the early prosperous days of the Ansteys. Each stage of four steps was covered by a strip of originally good but now worn and faded Wilton carpet secured by wooden stair rods. Parkin set to work systematically. He removed the carpet from the two lower stages of the staircase in turn and examined the steps in detail but without discovering anything of interest. He had just started on the third and final stage when he suddenly stiffened, subsiding on to his haunches and staring at a mark on the faded red wallpaper. It was a straight line running from the outer edge of the lowest step to that of the one immediately above it. Suppressing his excitement he took up the carpet and tried to prise up the tread of the lowest step. It was apparently immovable. A tense moment elapsed before he discovered two unobtrusive screws painted to match the dark oak.

'Ferris!' he shouted in a voice that brought Sergeant Ferris to his feet in a split second. 'Bring the tool kit.'

Within minutes they had cautiously removed the screws and were staring into a cavity. There was a slightly projecting nail in one corner around which was a trace of white powder . . .

Hardly daring to breathe and with infinite care Parkin got up the powder with the blade of a knife and transferred it to a sterilised container which he sealed and labelled. With Ferris's help the cavity was closed and screwed into place again and the staircarpet restored to its original position. Five minutes later the two men were heading for Highcastle, having urged the constables posted to keep the farm under observation to stay on their toes.

Within an hour of their return, Superintendent Bainbridge was in contact with a keenly interested senior officer of the Drugs Department at Scotland Yard, a laboratory test having confirmed that the white powder was heroin.

'Just the ticket on the top of the haul you people found on that chap who was killed last night,' the officer said with satisfaction. 'Of course the coastline in your part of the world's ideal for bringing the stuff in unobtrusively in smallish quantities. All those little holiday places and fishing boats coming and going ostensibly on their lawful occasions. Of course the important thing now is absolute secrecy. We're hoping to get on to the chaps who are behind the racket in a big way by keeping Anstey under obbo when he turns up.'

Superintendent Bainbridge asked if there were any further steps that the Drugs Department would like taken.

'You might have another look round in case there are any more dumps of the stuff somewhere else in the house. And the moment you hear from that travel agency of Anstey's that he's due back, get on to us, won't you?'

Superintendent Bainbridge undertook to co-operate in every possible way, including keeping a watch on Anstey's Farm round the clock. He rang off and turned to Inspector Parkin who had been following the conversation on an extension.

'Since you've got the hang of the place, you'd better finish the job,' he said. 'The building firm says their chaps will have done all the clearing up and installing safety measures they can by midday tomorrow, so you'd better go over after lunch and search what's left of the place. It was a damn good effort of yours, spotting that mark on the wallpaper.'

'Thank you, sir. Sergeant Ferris is spot on as a searcher. It was just chance that I took on the stairs while he vetted the stone flags of the hall floor. I'd like to take him along again tomorrow if he can be spared.'

'All right. Take him with you, but for God's sake get cracking. We've got enough on our plates without the ruddy arson at the place, let alone this drugs business on the top of it.'

'Thank you, sir,' Parkin replied with offical decorum.

On leaving the Super's office he tracked down Sergeant Ferris and they discussed their assignment over coffee in the canteen.

'There's the outbuildings and whatever,' Ferris said. 'Garage, oil stove, the well, the septic tank. The lot.'

Parkin thought it unlikely that any dope had been hidden outside the house as the dead man had been provided with a key.

'We've got to vet the whole bloody show, though,' he said. 'Let's try to make it by one o'clock. The builder's chaps ought to have cleared off well by then.'

'Should give us loads of time to get through by dark,' Ferris agreed. 'Barring something turning up out of the blue of course.'

High summer was continuing unbroken, and as they drove out to Anstey's Farm on schedule, Parkin and Ferris agreed that there was a lot to be said for a job that got you out into the country, given decent weather, even if it involved crawling about on filthy floors. Abandoning shop they discussed such matters as holiday plans and Parkin Junior's recent inclusion in his school's First Eleven.

On arrival they parked the police car out of sight behind the house. The two constables posted to keep the combe under observation emerged from the cover of trees and bushes. They reported that since they came out the only sign of life had been a hiking couple with rucksacks and a black labrador who had come up the road soon after the workmen had left at twelve. They had stood and stared at the house a bit, and then gone on up the path to Sinneldon and disappeared.

Bored by inaction the constables asked if they could lend a hand with the search.

'No way,' Parkin told them. 'Sorry, lads, but you're out here to keep obbo on the whole set-up. Count yourselves lucky that you're out of doors. Come on, Ferris, let's get cracking.'

55

It was immediately obvious from the encrusted moss and small weeds along their edges that the heavy cast iron covers of the well and septic tank had been undisturbed for a long period.

The garage and the paraffin store were both built of yellow bricks weathered to a drab beige. The firemen had replaced the broken padlock of the paraffin store with a new one and handed the key to the police. Parkin produced it and opened the door. In one corner on the concrete floor stood a large drum of paraffin fitted with a tap. In front of it were several containers capable of holding a couple of gallons each filled ready for use. A few empty containers were roughly stacked in the opposite corner. After satisfying themselves that the floor and brick walls were undisturbed they relocked the door and moved on to inspect the garage. This was a larger building with a work bench running down one side. On and under this was an untidy assortment of tools and materials useful for DIY jobs on a rather remote country property. There was a small pile of the yellow bricks covered with dust, half-empty bags of cement and sand, spare roofing tiles, a board with hardened mortar smeared on it, several half-empty tins of paint and various rusty tools, old buckets and similar workshop miscellanea. A ladder was propped against one of the walls with cobwebs hanging from it. A layer of dust over all these objects suggested that Paul Anstey was not addicted to DIY activities.

'Thank God the floor's concrete,' Parkin remarked. 'We'd better try out the walls for loose bricks, I suppose.'

Eventually satisfied that there were none of those, they relocked the garage and went into the house through the back door. After a sketchy wash at the scullery sink they debated which section of the house to tackle next and decided to start on the burnt out room at the far end.

The door from the hall into the first of the three rooms

had been barricaded to prevent unauthorised entry from the ruins into what remained of the house. Parkin and Ferris went outside and climbed through the empty rectangle formerly occupied by a window into the end room. It was open to the sky. Charred beams, rafters and roof tiles had been carried away by the workmen, but the floor was covered by a thick layer of unidentifiable burnt-up material in a soggy state from the damping-down activities of the firemen.

'God Almighty!' commented Ferris as he looked around. 'Do we clear all this muck ourselves so we can vet the flags?'

Parkin stood looking down at the fireplace in the back wall. The wooden partition boarding it up had been reduced to ashes, its disappearance exposing the brickwork which completely blocked off the space formerly occupied by a grate. Regardless of the state of the floor he dropped on to his knees and scrutinised the bricks and the crumbling mortar.

'Same as the ones outside,' he said, trying to ease a loose brick out as Ferris came and stood beside him.

It came away, bringing another with it. Parkin peered through the hole.

'There's something inside there,' he said, an oddly tense note in his voice as he wrenched further.

Quite suddenly several more bricks broke away together. There was an unidentifiable stealthy sound from the chimney as the long thin jointed fingers of a fleshless human hand came through the opening. Less hardened than Parkin, Ferris uttered a strangled blasphemy.

During the evening there was concentrated activity in the fire-ravaged end room at Anstey's Farm. . . . A police photographer recording every step of the investigation.

. . . Ghostly tapping of chisel on mortar as the ragged opening in the brickwork was carefully enlarged . . . Parkin and Ferris on their knees easing out the pathetically huddled and soot-stained skeleton, the right frontal area of the skull shattered, watched by Superintendent Bainbridge standing silently behind them, and gently depositing it on the waiting stretcher. . . . Its exit, the stretcher carried between two policemen to the van discreetly drawn up behind a clump of shrubs, the first stage on its journey to the forensic laboratory at Highcastle . . .

With its departure there was a relaxing of tension in the end room. Conversations began to be conducted in normal tones. Men in protective clothing began an investigation of the chimney with the help of powerful electric lamps. It proved unproductive. No clothing or other clues to the identify of the skeleton were found.

Overhead the ceiling and the greater part of the roof had collapsed but the bulk of the outer wall of solid granite blocks and the external chimney stack still stood. The former first floor room's fireplace had survived, and it could be seen from ground floor level that it, too, had been bricked up. There was a brief delay while a ladder was fetched. Parkin went up cautiously to investigate and reported that bricks of an identical type had been used. These, loosened by the fiercer heat of the fire on the more combustible first floor, were easily removed, and a search established that the draught-controlling damper in the chimney of the lower room had been closed and sealed with cement.

'Didn't miss a trick, the chap who fixed this job,' Superintendent Bainbridge, commented. 'There wasn't going to be any chance of a decomposing body making its presence felt upstairs.'

There was a further photographic session.

58

Finally the police cars left at ten-minute intervals, their headlights sweeping over the steep sides of the darkened combe, and two men remaining to keep the premises under observation as before.

'If people turn up they're much more likely to be newshounds of one sort or another than drug agents,' Parkin told them. 'Surprising they haven't got here already, come to that. God knows how they sniff out things the way they do. Just plug the investigation into the arson and say it's still going on for all you know.'

At Highcastle Police Headquarters a further conference was called after a hasty meal. The senior forensic scientist attended, clearly annoyed at having been forced to leave a fascinating post-mortem on the skeleton.

'All we can tell you people at this stage,' he told the assembled officers, 'is that the skeleton dates back at least twenty years and quite possibly a good deal longer. It's that of a male aged about 35 to 45, roughly five feet eight inches in height. Absolute accuracy of dating will be out of the question as you may already realise. We shall be analysing the mortar to get some idea of its age, of course.'

'Well, Super, what's your overall reaction?' the Chief Constable asked Bainbridge when the scientist had departed.

'Put it this way, sir,' came the reply. 'What we've got landed with is arson at an isolated house which is beyond any doubt involved in the drugs racket. It belongs to a chap whose comings and goings are a bit unusual, to say the least of it. We've now discovered deliberately concealed human remains on the premises dating back twenty years or more. As I see it pretty extensive enquiries'll be needed to clear up the business, and we just haven't the resources to make 'em.'

'You mean you think it's a case for calling in the Yard?'

59

'Just that, sir.'

'Hard luck on you,' the CC said, turning to Parkin. 'You've done damn well on the job so far.'

'It makes sense, sir,' Parkin replied sturdily. 'I can see for myself. I couldn't make the going from now on, the way things have turned out.'

'What you've done won't be forgotten, Parkin. You can count on that.... Well, I suppose we go ahead.... It was before my time and yours, Super, but it was that Yard ace Pollard, wasn't it, who pulled off that case at Affacombe? No harm in asking if he's available for this one....

Chapter 6

'Come in and sit down,' said the Assistant Commissioner as Detective-Chief Superintendent Tom Pollard appeared in his office on the following morning in response to a summons. He selected a file from a number on his desk. 'Naturally, since you got yourself involved in the arson enquiry at this Anstey's Farm place, Highcastle are yelling for you to take over the latest development there. I take it you've seen the papers and know what I'm talking about?'

'The Skeleton in the Chimney, sir?' Pollard queried.

'Yes. Highcastle have dug up that case of yours at Affacombe in their area, and they're dwelling at length on what an advantage it is to an investigating officer to know the district. By the way, how long ago was this Affacombe business?'

'Good Lord, sir! About sixteen years. I'd barely cut my eye teeth. Good old Super Crowe propelled me through it somehow.'

'Great chap, Crowe,' the AC agreed. 'Still is. I hear he's still in the Polharbour Bowls Club team. Now then, about this SOS from Highcastle. One's got to admit that there are some odd features about the case. On the face of it you're going down to find out who bashed in a man's

61

head and bricked up his body in a chimney at Anstey's Farm at least twenty years ago according to the Highcastle forensics' timing. There is also absolute proof that the house has been used in the heroin distribution network. Highcastle have unearthed a concealed hiding place and unmistakable traces of the stuff on the premises. They say that it's impossible to see how this could have been organised without Paul Anstey's knowledge and co-operation, and no doubt he's doing nicely out of it. Rather suggestively he owns and runs a travel agency just off the Tottenham Court Road called *Going Places*. He pays fairly frequent irregular visits to the farm, staying a night or two. The Drugs Squad propose to take their time. Anstey's in the States at the moment alleged to be planning future tours for his clientele. The DS don't propose to nab him at Heathrow. Their idea is that if he thinks nobody's tumbled to the heroin racket he'll resume operations after a bit, and they'll get him red-handed and some of his associates as well. Ostensibly Highcastle are trying to get him back in connection with the arson. And another odd feature of the case is the arson itself, of course. You're officially going down to clear up the skeleton in the chimney murder, but Highcastle and the DS will be damn grateful if you can sort out the heroin and the arson *en passant*. And it's a bit much to accept that an isolated farmhouse should have been the scene of three unrelated serious crimes.'

'If,' Pollard said, 'the forensic chaps are right about the skeleton being at least twenty years old, it looks as though there'll have to be a fair bit of digging up the past. . . . I can have Toye, I take it, sir? And get some other chaps on to necessary enquiries up here?'

'As long as you don't get the idea that you can both spend the rest of your lives down at this bloody farm,' the AC replied. 'The homicide rate over the country at large

62

is rising steadily. Here, take this. Highcastle sent some-body up with it overnight. All the gen's in it, updated to last night. As usual, you're landed an interesting case. Good hunting, and keep in touch, that's all.'

Pollard fielded the folder, gave assurances of frequent contact and extricated himself. By the time he reached his own office a course of action had already taken shape in his mind. A call to the Office Manager of *Going Places* established that Mr Paul Anstey had not rung in for the past forty-eight hours.

'You may not know,' Pollard told him, 'that Scotland Yard has taken over the enquiry into the discovery of human remains at Mr Anstey's farm. I am now officially in charge. When Mr Anstey next calls you, please ask him to contact me immediately, either at the Yard or at Highcastle police station. Here are the two numbers . . .' As he dictated them he sensed a degree of agitation at the other end of the line. With the FBI he was more explicit, and given every assurance that Paul Anstey would be quickly located, informed that Scotland Yard urgently required his presence in connection with an enquiry into an apparent homicide at Anstey's Farm, and kept under observation. A third call asked for a confidential report on Martin Anstey from the Cape Town branch of Randall's, the London-based publishing firm.

All these matters having been put in hand to his satisfaction, he buzzed his secretary.

'Ask Inspector Toye to come along, will you?' he said.

The two men had worked closely together for over twenty years and had developed an intimate knowledge of the functioning of each other's minds. Physically and psycho-logically they presented a marked contrast. At fifty Poll-ard was tall, well-built and fair with only a few grey touches in his hair. His mental alertness and determination were not immediately apparent in his open pleasant face, a fact which Jane Pollard often remarked was one of his major assets as a CID man. Gregory Toye, five years older, only just achieved the regulation minimal height, with dark hair receding from a pale impassive face. By temperament he was conservative and cautious, and a perfect foil to the more pragmatic Pollard whom he still secretly hero-worshipped after two decades of exacting co-operation in many demanding and sometimes dangerous situations. On this occasion, as Pollard had expected, he listened to a precis of the Anstey's Farm case with the air of one who foresees serious, if not insoluble problems.

'Three cases for the price of one, I call it,' he commented when Pollard had finished.

'This is it,' he agreed. 'The obvious first step is to decide on our course of action. Here, let's have some grub sent up from the canteen and work through all this gen while we're eating.'

By mid-afternoon they had agreed that as a starting point the skeleton had its limitations.

'The Highcastle forensics are cagey, as you'd expect.' Pollard said. 'They only commit themselves to the extent of saying that the thing had been in the chimney for not less than twenty years. So what? Thirty years? Forty? Fifty? And to be even more helpful they add that they can never be 100% accurate about it.'

'Raises no end of problems,' Toye observed gloomily. 'Who owned the farm or was living in it when the job was done? It mightn't have been this travel agency chap at all.'

'According to Highcastle the Ansteys have been living there for several generations. We've simply got to delve into their family history.'

'Go down there right away, you mean?'

'The Registrar of births, marriages and deaths at Highcastle,' Pollard said thoughtfully. 'Chatting up local

64

people. . . . No, I've got a better idea than that, to start with, anyway. Martin Anstey, Paul's nephew, who works at Randall's, the publishers.'

'He's lived all his life in Africa till a few months ago,' Toye objected.

'He must have known something about his family to have tried to contact his uncle at the farm. Anyway, we shall get a certain amount of info out of him, so we shan't be starting from scratch when we get down there.' Pollard dialled the Yard's switchboard and asked to be put through to Randall's, the publishers.

Within an unexpectedly short space of time Martin Anstey announced himself over the line. Pollard registered fleetingly that it was a pleasing voice with just the faintest trace of un-English clipped vowels and drawl.

'This is Detective-Chief Superintendent Pollard speaking from New Scotland Yard, Mr Anstey,' he said. 'Can I take it that you know that a human skeleton with a shattered skull has been discovered in a chimney at Anstey's Farm, your uncle Mr Paul Anstey's house?'

'You can,' Martin Anstey replied. 'Inspector Parkin rang me from Highcastle last night. It's – well, a bit difficult to take in, somehow.'

'I can understand that,' Pollard said. 'Rather fantastic, in fact, isn't it? Why I'm ringing you now is that we want what help you can give us. Did Inspector Parkin tell you that forensic experts are prepared to state definitely, even at this early stage, that the skeleton has been bricked up in that chimney for at least twenty years and possibly quite a bit longer?'

'Yes, he did.'

'Then it will be obvious to you that we must establish who has been the official occupier of the farm over the past forty years, say. We have not so far managed to get in touch with Mr Paul Anstey, and felt it was worth trying

65

you, even though we understand that you have spent your whole life in Zimbabwe and South Africa up to a few months ago. Have you any information that could be helpful to us?'

There was a pause.

'I'm not all that keen on this,' Martin Anstey said slowly, 'even if one of my forebears *was* a murderer. Not that I knew any of them personally. Except my father, of course. He emigrated in 1945, as soon as he was demobbed after World War Two.'

'At the moment there's absolutely no evidence that any member of the Anstey family committed this murder,' Pollard replied. 'There are other important matters to investigate. For instance, was the farm let at any time during the past forty years, and if so, who was the tenant? Or was it left empty for any considerable period for some reason? This is the kind of information we need urgently, and we thought you might be able to clear up points of this sort in the absence of the present owner.'

'Well, I get you,' Martin said. 'All right. I'm prepared to pass on anything I know. All hearsay from my father, of course. As a matter of fact it's just struck me that somebody who probably knows a lot more than I do about what's happened to the farm in the last half-century or so is my fiancée, Gemma Ford. She's the niece by marriage of Maynard Hooper, the owner of the Peatcutters Inn at Dollaford, and often stays down there. I've gathered from her that my sudden appearance last weekend sparked off reminiscences without end about the family. Would it be useful if I got her round to my flat this evening to tell you anything she picked up?'

'From what I know of villages and village pubs it could be very helpful indeed,' Pollard told him. 'We'd be most grateful to her.'

'OK, then. I'll knock off early and hunt out various

papers of my father's that I brought back from South Africa. There's a family tree, I remember, back to when the Ansteys made a killing over selling their farm in the Midlands to a railway company back in the middle of the last century. Shall we say about eight-thirty? You have my address and telephone number, I take it? I've got a bachelor pad off Baker Street.'

'We have. And many thanks, Mr Anstey, for your co-operation.'

'W.1, just,' Pollard remarked as he stood with Toye looking up at a recently-built block of small flats overlooking gardens. 'Not cheap. Martin Anstey must be moderately well-heeled to live here.'

A couple of minutes later they arrived at the door of Flat 17 on the second floor. In answer to their ring it was opened by a tall dark young man with an intelligent face wearing massive horn-rimmed spectacles.

'Do come in,' he said. 'Detective-Chief Superintendent Pollard, I take it, and . . .?'

'My assistant, Inspector Toye,' Pollard told him.

They were ushered into a large room on the right of the narrow passage which apparently ran the depth of the flat. Pollard had an exceptional ability for rapidly sizing up his surroundings. It was a surprisingly spacious room, its big window at the far end looking out on the gardens and beyond them over a panorama of assorted roofs. In a flash Pollard registered a flat-topped desk with neat stacks of papers and books, well-filled bookcases, comfortable chairs and some eye-catching landscapes on the walls vigorously expressing wide sweeps of country in interesting colour. South Africa, obviously, he thought, going forward to meet the girl who had got up from a chair and taken a step towards him.

'Chief Superintendent Pollard, darling,' Martin

67

Anstey said, 'and Inspector Toye. Both of the Yard. . . . My fiancée Superintendent, Miss Gemma Ford.'

'This is quite a moment,' Gemma said as they shook hands. 'This is the sort of thing that happens to other people. I never thought that I'd meet anyone from such an eminence. Do sit down.'

In the momentary upheaval of organising a group of four chairs Pollard gathered an impression of charm without striking good looks, personality and a quality of openness and integrity.

'Believe me, Miss Ford,' he told her as they sat down, 'we're just a bunch of very ordinary chaps at the Yard who suffer from the Sherlock Holmes mystique dreamed up by Conan Doyle.'

'Don't shatter our illusions,' Martin Anstey said, producing a folder. 'Anyway, one thing I'm sure of is that you've no time to waste, so I've dug out the few family papers I brought back. There's nothing much – Dad emigrated as soon as he could after being demobbed in 1945 and brought precious little out with him. Here's a rather primitive family tree he made out to show me when I was a kid.'

'I like the comments,' Pollard remarked after studying the document. 'May Inspector Toye make a copy of the essentials? . . . No, please don't bother,' he added as Martin Anstey made a move to fetch writing materials. 'We're all equipped with the well-known regulation notebook. It's been very helpful to see this family tree of yours, Mr Anstey. Clearly we needn't go back beyond your grandfather. As he inherited the farm in 1910, that's seventy-four years ago, almost four times the Highcastle forensic scientists' tentative estimate of the skeleton's age. Would he have been literally farming from this time on?'

'Yes. At that stage there was quite a bit of land, both in the combe and up on Sinneldon.'

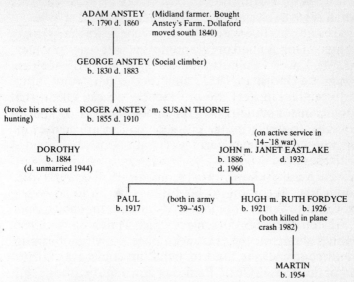

ADAM ANSTEY (Midland farmer. Bought
b. 1790 d. 1860   Anstey's Farm. Dollaford
                   moved south 1840)

GEORGE ANSTEY (Social climber)
b. 1830 d. 1883

(broke his neck out   ROGER ANSTEY m. SUSAN THORNE
hunting)   b. 1855 d. 1910

                                        (on active service in
                                         '14–'18 war)
        DOROTHY   JOHN m. JANET EASTLAKE
        b. 1884   b. 1886   d. 1932
        (d. unmarried 1944)   d. 1960

        PAUL   (both in army   HUGH m. RUTH FORDYCE
        b. 1917   '39–'45)   b. 1921   b. 1926
                                    (both killed in plane
                                    crash 1982)

                                    MARTIN
                                    b. 1954

'What happened to the house and the land when he joined up in 1914?'

'His unmarried elder sister came and took over for the duration.'

'So the house was occupied by your great-aunt until your grandfather came back in 1918 or early 1919?'

Martin Anstey grinned.

'She walked out for good on the morning of his return with a wife. Melodramatic perhaps, but one can see that she might reasonably feel that she'd had a raw deal after running the show extremely well, apparently, for four years.'

Gemma glanced up.

'Public opinion seems to have been on her side. I heard two elderly farmers discussing it in the bar after Martin had gone. According to them she only knew that John had married a couple of days earlier.'

69

'According to my father,' Martin took up, 'she was the boss-woman to end all boss-women. Highly capable but impossible to live with. Obviously there wasn't going to be room for her and my grandmother in the same house.'

'Well, well,' Pollard said. 'I see that your Uncle Paul had been born in 1917, and that Hugh, your father followed on in 1921. So presumably we can take it that John Anstey settled down on demobilisation to a spell of family life and farming. You see that I'm still on the tack of whether Anstey's Farm was continuously occupied at this stage.'

'As far as I know it was, from late 1918 or early 1919 onwards. According to Dad things began to go wrong towards the end of the 1920s. My grandfather had money invested in foreign currencies which went west, and farm prices slumped, too. He more or less gave up farming, sold nearly all the land for what he could get and just kept the house. Uncle Paul was down for Oxbridge, but that was off, and my grandfather found him a job in a London insurance company. He was simply rabid, apparently, walked out on it, and nothing more was heard of him until the Highcastle solicitors managed to track him down after grandfather's death. My grandmother had died from pneumonia in 1932. Dad was eleven, and at Polharbour Grammar School. Life was pretty depressing for him, and he used to say that he had been quite glad when World War Two broke out and he joined up and got away. He was fond of Anstey's Farm, though, and hoped to buy out Uncle Paul and live there himself when he retired.'

'Did your grandfather stay on there?'

'As far as I know he never left it until he died in 1960. My father was demobbed in 1945, went back to Anstey's while he fixed up his emigration, but in the end never saw the place again.'

Pollard turned to Gemma.

'Does the chat you've heard in the Peatcutters throw any light on whether John Anstey ever let the farm or shut it up for long periods, Miss Ford?'

'I've never heard anybody talk about his letting the place or being away for any length of time,' Gemma replied. 'As far as I've gathered he lived out there on his own, just coming into Dollaford to shop and have a drink at the Peatcutters. Oh, yes, he had a car of sorts: a proper old rattletrap somebody said, so I suppose he could have gone into Highcastle or Polharbour or even been further afield. And a Dollaford woman went over to clean now and again.'

'What about Paul Anstey since he inherited the place?' Pollard asked her.

'He's not liked, and personally I haven't heard him discussed much. I've gathered that it's generally felt that he behaved badly to his father and there's still indignation that he didn't turn up for the funeral. And some resentment, I gather from my uncle, that he just uses the farm as a *pied à terre* instead of living there and offering a job or two to the locals. I'm quite sure that I've never heard of him letting it. My uncle might know, as far as the last eight years go.'

'He comes down for an odd night or two fairly frequently, I gather?'

'That's my impression,' Gemma Ford replied. 'Of course I'm not down at Dollaford all that much myself. He comes down chiefly to see his dog, I think.'

'His *dog*?'

'Yes. Apparently he was driving down from London some years ago, and some absolutely foul people in a car in front of him chucked out a puppy they wanted to get rid of and drove on at speed. He rescued it, and it's a permanent boarder at a kennels called *Dogdays* on

71

Crownmoor. He goes over to see it. Miss Pettinger who runs the place would know much more about his comings and goings than I do.'

There was a short pause during which Pollard considered the information he had gathered. Obviously John Anstey had been a pretty ruthless type, and there must have been days on end when he was alone in what seemed to be an unusually remote house. . . . Suppose an inquisitive stranger had turned up?

'What was the cause of your grandfather's death?' he asked Martin.

'A coronary. He died in his sleep, and was found by the woman Gemma was talking about when she next went over to clean and so on.'

'Do you know how long it was before Mr Paul Anstey was traced and took possession of the house?'

'Not offhand, but the solicitor's letters to my father who'd always kept in touch with grandfather are in this folder. I was only a small kid at the time but my father talked about it all sometimes, and my impression is that it was several months anyway. You'll want to take the folder, I expect?'

'You can be sure that it'll be taken care of and returned to you,' Pollard told him. 'Make out an official receipt, Inspector, will you, and then we'll remove ourselves.'

While waiting he chatted easily with Martin and Gemma. Not only likeable but a lot to them, he thought, asking when they were getting married.

'As soon as we can find somewhere possible to live,' Martin told him. 'It isn't all that easy, as I'm sure you know.'

'Interesting,' Pollard observed, 'that you should meet up here in London and find you both had a link with the Dollaford area.'

His remark was greeted with silence, and he looked up to find the couple eyeing him a little doubtfully but with suppressed amusement.

'Come on, let's tell him,' Gemma said, her blue eyes dancing. 'We first met a week ago today, Chief Superintendent.'

'At the Peatcutters,' Martin added. 'And that was that.'

'I expect you think we're obviously dotty,' Gemma suggested, 'and are wondering how reliable our statements are.'

'On the contrary,' Pollard assured her, 'you've made our day. Haven't they, Inspector?' he asked Toye who had joined them, receipt in hand, his normally solemn face transformed by a beaming smile. 'He's a romantic at heart in spite of the depressing nature of most of our work.'

Toye decorously wished the couple every happiness in their future life together and added that their news had made the day stand out all right.

'After this heartening glimpse of love at first sight,' Pollard said as they drove back to the Yard, 'we'd better just call to mind what we made this call for and where we'd better go from here.'

They agreed that on the face of it John Anstey and his son Paul had both apparently had the opportunity to murder the unknown man and stow away his body, but that the odds seemed to be on John.

'All those years living on his own in the place,' Toye said. 'Do we go down and see what we can get out of the locals?'

'This is it. I'll get on to Highcastle and fix a meeting for tomorrow which won't be exactly popular seeing it's Saturday. Let's face it, this job looks like being a long drawn-out and bloody difficult affair. Clues over twenty years old and everyone saying that what we're asking about was before their time.'

Toye characteristically agreed with this pessimistic outlook. On returning to his office, however, Pollard found that there had been at least one satisfactory development. Paul Anstey had been located by the FBI and had undertaken to fly back on the following Tuesday.

'Looks as though he's banking on the skeleton diverting attention from the drugs racket,' Toye suggested. 'Natural enough for him to go out to inspect the fire damage and the chimney and to take the opportunity of clearing out the heroin dump he'd expect to find.'

'My guess is that practically as soon as he gets back he'll be told by somebody in the heroin racket that the chap bringing that last lot in was killed on the road, and that the police would have found the heroin on him. What he won't know, though, is about the diagram the poor devil was unwise enough to carry on him.'

'Should have memorised it,' Toye observed, being exceptionally thorough.

'Good thing you never took to crime yourself,' Pollard commented.

Chapter 7

Pollard was accustomed to being received with varying degrees of chilliness by police authorities who had reluctantly felt obliged to call in the Yard to handle a case. On presenting himself with Toye at Highcastle on the following morning he was agreeably surprised at being welcomed with undisguised relief.

'We've no sooner started working on one crime at that bloody Anstey's Farm than we're up to the neck in another,' the Chief Constable complained with exasperation over mid-morning coffee. 'We haven't even traced the chaps who ran down the bloke who had the heroin on him. Over to you, Chief Superintendent and I wish you luck. Inspector Parkin's done some first-rate work on the job, but we just can't cope with all the ramifications it keeps sprouting on the top of our normal workload. What price that crazy business of a chap dancing on the edge of the combe at daybreak?'

Pollard was sympathetic and also complimentary on the contents of Inspector Parkin's case file.

'We've already made contact over the phone,' he said, 'and I hope we may call on him for the sort of help we're going to need, anyway until we've taken in the lie of the land and who's who.'

Having reassured him on this point and on the availability of manpower for routine enquiries and similar jobs the Chief Constable departed, leaving Superintendent Bainbridge and Inspector Parkin to hand over the case. The Super, Pollard learnt, had only taken over at Highcastle a couple of months previously and appeared somewhat weighed down by unfamiliar responsibilities. Parkin, a younger man, was obviously intelligent and competent, and secretly revelling in being involved in what had become a widely publicised case, hitting the headlines.

According to Superintendent Bainbridge there was very little to report beyond lack of progress on all fronts. The identity of the man accidentally killed en route to Anstey's Farm with heroin had not so far been established. One of the men who operated a motor launch service between Polharbour and the larger port of Kings Quay farther along the coast had come forward in response to the description put out by the police. He was taken to Highcastle General Hospital, but on being shown the body said that he could not definitely swear that this was a man he had taken on board at Kings Quay on the afternoon of Tuesday, 19 June. Other reports of the dead man having been seen at Polharbour had been followed up but without any satisfactory outcome.

In spite of exhaustive enquiries no evidence had come to light about vandals at large in the Sinnel valley area on the night of the arson at Anstey's Farm, nor of the man whose antics had been observed on the very early morning of 18 June by Fireman Forches on standby duty after the fire. Nothing had come from enquiries about mentally unstable persons living in the area. No steps had been taken to trace the author of the anonymous letter to the police about Martin Anstey's car being parked on the main road near the track up to the farm on the morning of 16 June.

'It didn't seem important,' Bainbridge said, 'and we just haven't got round to it. Glove prints but no identifiable dabs to be checked with our records, and no further letters. A pretty obvious nutcase from the look of it.'

As Pollard made no comment, he went on to discuss the forensic laboratory's final report on the age of the skeleton and the state of the mortar used in the bricking-up of the two fireplaces. The scientists carrying out the investigation had not altered their original estimate of a period of twenty years or possibly more and they were not prepared to commit themselves beyond giving it as their unanimous opinion that the murder had been committed between twenty and thirty years earlier. The skeleton was that of a man in normal health aged between thirty-five and forty-five. Death had been due to a violent blow which had shattered the occipital bone of the skull. A careful record had been made of dental work carried out at various stages in the life of the deceased, and circulation of this among members of the dental profession could be helpful in establishing his identity, but it was bound to be a slow job. Literally thousands of printed replicas of the dead man's dental record had been circulated to dental practices with an urgent request for co-operation.

The timing estimate, in the view of Superintendent Bainbridge, could hardly make things more difficult, focusing the enquiry on the decade 1954–1964. John Anstey's doctor was still alive and had been interviewed. He stated that his late patient had been an unusually fit and active man for his age, whose sudden death from a coronary thrombosis had taken place in November 1960. He gave it as his opinion that John Anstey would have been perfectly capable of bashing in another man's head and carrying out the job in the chimney at any time between 1954 and 1960.

Inspector Parkin had investigated the delay in Paul Anstey's arrival at the farm after his father's death. Most unfortunately, John Anstey's solicitor who had carried out the task of tracing Paul had himself died recently, but his partners had been most helpful in providing what information they could. Paul had eventually been located at a winter sports centre in Switzerland where he was organising skiing holidays. He had come down to Highcastle to hear the terms of his father's Will, and for a time at least had been in residence at Anstey's Farm. Hugh Anstey, formerly resident in Southern Rhodesia, had been kept informed of these facts.

'So the place was shut up for about a couple of months,' Superintendent Bainbridge commented. 'In the depth of winter with precious few people going up on to the moor. Pretty well anything could have been going on there, although it's true that there's no record of a break-in during the period. And this is the sum total of what we've got on offer, Mr Pollard. Damn all, let's face it.'

'Far from it, Super,' Pollard replied. 'We now know the two periods during which the murder could have been carried out, unobserved and at leisure, so to speak, assuming that the forensic chaps have got their dating right. One is from 1954 to John Anstey's death in November 1960. During these years he was living alone at the farm and is obviously a potential suspect. There follows the time before Paul returns: November 1960 to February 1961, during which the farm was shut up. It seems highly improbable, but in theory somebody unconnected with the family could have broken into the house and used it as a handy place for disposing of a corpse. Finally, Paul Anstey lived there for an unspecified period after returning in February 1961, probably on his own judging from his current life-style when in residence there. Were

78

there any unexplained local disappearances in the area between '54 and '64?'

'Not one, sir,' Parkin replied. 'One of the first things we did was to go through the records.'

'On the whole,' Pollard said, 'all this seems to me to tip the scales in favour of Paul as the murderer. He must have had outside contacts, while I gather that John became more or less a recluse in his later years. I suppose there are no records of any breach of the peace between either one of them and some local inhabitant?'

'None,' Bainbridge replied. 'We've checked on that, too.'

'Thanks. Well, the moment seems to have arrived for us to start on a spot of ferreting ourselves, although exactly what for I'm anything but clear so far. I think a visit to the scene of the crime is as good a starting point as any.'

'We've booked you rooms at the Southgate. How about going along there and checking in, having a snack, then coming back here to collect Parkin? He can follow you out to the farm, show you the lie of the land and leave you to it.'

The Southgate had been updated and acquired an additional star since Pollard and Toye had stayed there during their case at Affacombe sixteen years earlier. Pollard found that he rememberd the hotel quite clearly. The case had been only his second big one, and memories of the tension and frustrations he had experienced came back to him as he downed a snack and some lager in the now rather grandiose bar. He was visited by a sudden vivid recollection of a dream he had had, and from which the night porter had roused him to take a call from the Yard. . . . A remark from Toye that a mint of money had been spent on the place and quite spoilt the

79

look of it recalled him to the present.

Parkin, clearly in his element at this chance to cooperate with the Yard, was waiting with one of the Highcastle cars when they returned to police headquarters. He led the way through the city to the road following the Sinnel valley along which Pollard and Jane had driven Londonwards a week earlier. As they took the turning to Affacombe Pollard wondered briefly what Olivia Strode was doing and if there would be any chance of contacting her during the days ahead. After another five miles Parkin signalled a right turn, slowed down and negotiated a narrow bridge over the Sinnel which led to a grassy track. Toye followed with a muttered protest at having to hazard his cherished Rover on an unsurfaced road. Fascinated, Pollard watched the setting of the events recorded in the file of the case unfolding before his eyes. The track bore left and the combe began to narrow rapidly with trees flooding down its sides. Involuntarily his eyes moved to its far end where Sinneldon, the bastion of Crownmoor, reared up and formed a seemingly impassable barrier. Then his gaze dropped to the cluster of buildings on a grassy terrace to the right of the stream. Roughly half the principal one, the long-house which he had contemplated with Jane, was a burnt out wreck. The other half was badly stained by smoke but still standing with its ground floor windows still shuttered and its front door apparently intact. Behind the house were two intact brick-built sheds.

Parkin drew up smartly at the front door and leapt out to release Pollard from the Rover.

'All yours, sir,' he said. 'Looks a bit different to what it was when you and your lady were on holiday, I reckon.'

'Bad business,' Pollard commented. 'There are precious few of these old long-houses left. Take us on an escorted tour, will you, Inspector? Round the outside first, to get a general idea of the layout.'

Parkin conducted them round the undamaged end of the farm to the paraffin store and the garage. Here he pointed out the pile of bricks identical with the samples taken from the chimney in which the skeleton had been bricked up.

'There was a trowel with the mortar hardened on it,' he told them. 'The lab chaps analysed that too, and found the cement was identical with the stuff in that sack there.'

They moved on round the back of the farm to the burnt north-eastern section. The shutters of the two windows of the larger living room were charred and the glass behind them was broken. At the far end only the aperture formerly occupied by the window of the smaller room remained. Pollard rested his hands on the sill and contemplated the bare space inside open to the sky.

'If you'd been planning to burn down this place where would you have started the fire?' he asked Parkin and Toye.

Both men agreed that they would have gone for the middle so that the flames could have spread in both directions. Parkin pointed out that access to the hall would have been difficult unless the arsonist had a key to the front door, which presumably he hadn't.

'The window of the bigger room next to the hall would have been the best place to pour the paraffin in to my mind,' he said.

'Seems to me,' Toye suggested, 'that there was less risk of being spotted at the far end from anyone coming down the track from the top as you and Mrs Pollard did, sir.'

'I suppose there are moonlight walkers on the moor in the summer,' Pollard said. 'I know I'd like to be one myself. But surely the path my wife and I were on before we turned off down this combe goes on, and anyone following it would be able to look straight down on this end of the house? Isn't it just there that the fireman saw a chap capering about at daybreak last Monday?'

Parkin agreed, adding that he had never been up there himself, and that his impression was that the route down the combe was more used than the continuation of the track along Sinneldon.

'We're so clueless at the moment that when we've had a look at your star turn on the stairs, Parkin, I'd like you two to go up and check on how much can be seen of this end of the house from the path that goes on towards Affacombe, and if there's any trace of the dancing bloke.'

Highly gratified, Parkin led the way to the back door, unlocked it and escorted Pollard and Toye to the scene of his breakthrough on the stairs. The stair rods of the third flight of steps were removed, the carpet folded back, the concealed screws extracted and the cavity displayed.

'Nifty of you to have tumbled to the significance of that mark on the wall,' Pollard remarked.

He contemplated the cavity for so long that when he looked up he found Parkin eyeing him in unspoken enquiry.

'Just how big was that trickle of spilt heroin you got out of here?' he asked.

Parkin considered.

'Say a level teaspoonful, sir. Just a thin trickle running from where the head of that nail just sticks out to about here.' He indicated the side of the cavity.

'It looks to me,' Pollard said thoughtfully, 'that somebody cleared out this cache of the muck in a hurry. Anstey went back to London last Monday week. No reason to suppose that he was in a tearing hurry. So what?'

Toye suggested that a fresh lot of heroin had been dumped a few days after Paul's departure, and that when the news of the fire got round one of the members of the

82

local drugs network acted promptly to remove the stuff.

'If you'll excuse me, sir,' Parkin put in, 'there wouldn't have been much chance to organise removing the stuff. The Fire Service had a couple of men on duty over the Sunday night and all through Monday. June the seventeenth that was. We're shorthanded, and the Super cancelled the cover for the Monday night, but that was the night when the chap who was bringing in a consignment of heroin was run down and killed. He didn't die till the early hours of Tuesday morning, and the Super sent out another couple of chaps by eight o'clock. I don't say it couldn't have been done, but it would have taken a bit of time for the news to get round to somebody in on the racket who could have got to the farm and cleared out this hide, and pushed off again without being seen before our chaps came on duty at eight o'clock.'

'You've certainly got a point there, Parkin,' Pollard agreed. 'All the same, when you're as up against it as we all are over this complex mess, it's advisable to keep every possible relevant point in mind. X in a hurry, in this instance. . . . Anyway, Toye, you and I simply must remember that we're officially on the murder enquiry, not on the arson or the drug running. I'll have another potter round while you two go up to the top and scrounge around.'

Left alone, Pollard returned to the room where the skeleton had been disposed of and the fire started. He inspected the chimney again, but convinced that he could learn nothing new from it he climbed out again and made his way to the terrace in front of the house. Flinging himself down on the grass he faced the fact that he had seldom, if ever, been confronted with a more intractable case. The one advantage it offered was its restricted geographical setting: Anstey's Farm and its neighbourhood. John Anstey's grave was in Dollaford churchyard.

The anonymous letter about Martin Anstey's car must have been written by someone who had seen it in Dollaford, probably in the Peatcutters' car park. The Highcastle police had completely failed to trace any strange cars containing potential arsonists in the area on the night of the fire. It was partly the time factor that made things so baffling. The murder of the unknown thirty to forty years ago. . . . Paul Anstey apparently off stage from the mid-thirties to early 1961. . . . Martin Anstey only appearing in the UK a few months ago. . . . Hell! Were the Ansteys involved in the murder at all?

Absently picking a piece of rye grass Pollard began to chew it as he meditated on the Ansteys. John, from all accounts, had been a pretty unpleasant old tough, certainly in his dealings with his sister and probably with his eldest son. Paul seemed to have repaid him in the same coin. There was something particularly ruthless in keeping up the breach with his father all through the war, and afterwards. What was he doing in the years between being demobbed and 1961 when he was run to earth to be told that his father had died? It struck Pollard that so far he had given very little thought to this period of Paul's life, and enquiries must be got going as quickly as possible. . . . His thoughts moved on to Martin Anstey. It seemed hardly credible that anyone living in the Dollaford area could have had time and opportunity to develop strong personal animosity towards him. So what? Could there possibly be some sort of deep-rooted local vendetta against the whole Anstey family?

At this point uneven footfalls on broken ground became audible, and distant voices heralded the return of Toye and Parkin. Pollard began to catch glimpses of them as they came down the path that he and Jane had followed so recently. Finally they came out of the trees, headed for the footbridge and scrambled up the slope to join him. He was immediately aware that something had been achieved and grinned at them.

'Reasonably comfortable here,' he said, and they flung themselves down beside him.

'Well, sir,' Parkin began, 'to start with the actual path is well back from the edge of the combe, and walking along towards Affacombe you can't see the farm at all until you've nearly got round the head of the combe, so to speak. You come to a gap in the trees just there – see? . . . Well, that must be the place where the fireman saw the bloke capering about. We went to the edge and found signs of the grass being trampled, didn't we, Inspector? You carry on from here.'

'We kept to one side,' Toye took up, 'and right near the edge there's a clump of bracken with some of the stems snapped off making a bit of a hollow in the middle. We took a look in it and found these bits and pieces.'

He produced the outer wrapping of a Mars bar, two apple cores and a couple of banana skins.

'Then nearer the edge,' he went on, 'we picked up this.' He held out a small dog biscuit of a well-known brand. 'I reckon the chap pulled it out of his pocket with the handkerchief the report says he was waving.'

'Paul Anstey's got a dog he boards permanently at some kennels near here,' Pollard said, contemplating the find. 'Martin Anstey's girlfriend told us about it. Remember? I wonder if there's a possible link-up with this three-headed case of ours? Anyway, it suggests a job for tomorrow. We'll go and call at the kennels and find out if anyone on the strength might have been the fireman's dancer at daybreak. Meanwhile we'll go and have a look at Dollaford and then I shall feel I've got the hang of the lie of the land, anyway.'

After Parkin had departed for Highcastle, Pollard and Toye duly turned right for Dollaford. Pollard glanced at his watch.

'Just on six on a Saturday evening,' he said. 'The pub will be filling up, and I've got a nasty feeling that the local press and media may have got on to our takeover, and even worse, that my dial may have been displayed to their readers and viewers. I'll go and look at the church. There's always somewhere to park outside a country church. Meanwhile you go and have a look round the village. I'm interested in the pub's car park if it has one. And also if there are paths leading up on to Sinneldon from the village.'

They parked unobtrusively by a lychgate from which a path led to the south porch of a small church. Pollard contemplated the exterior with interest, detecting some Early English features and later rebuilding in the fifteenth century. He tried the door, found it unlocked and went inside. The interior was beautifully kept and he wandered round, examining the carved bench ends and traces of wall-paintings. There was a peal of five bells, the ringing chamber being at ground level at the base of the tower. A series of plaques commemorated the ringing of special peals on particular occasions, and a brass plate recorded the recasting of the bells in 1865 through the generosity of George Anstey, Esq. of Anstey's Farm, Dollaford. As Pollard was studying this and placing George as Martin's great-great-grandfather, he heard footsteps coming up the path. The south door opened and a woman came in carrying a few flowers and a pair of sécateurs.

'Good evening,' he said, coming forward. 'I expect you want to lock up? I was driving through the village and thought I'd stop to have a quick look round if the church were still open. How beautifully it's kept.'

He placed the woman in her fifties. She had a pleasant face and a fresh country complexion and was wearing a workaday cotton skirt and blouse. She was carrying flowers and a pair of sécateurs in a trug.

86

'No need to hurry yourself, sir. I didn't get the flowers for tomorrow finished this morning and I've just slipped over now. I'm glad you think we keep the church nice. We do what we can but it's a bit of a struggle these days.'

'Smaller congregation?' he asked.

'Partly that. Folk don't come to church the way they used to, and there just doesn't seem to be the money around. And we haven't a proper vicar. Only the Sinnel Valley Group Ministry.'

'I suppose at one time there were well-to-do people in the neighbourhood who helped keep up the church? I was looking at a brass plate when you came in which said a Mr George Anstey once paid for the bells to be recast.'

'That's right. Long before my time, of course. Out at Anstey's Farm, he lived, off the Affacombe road. Decent enough folk then the Ansteys were, but they've brought nothing but shame to Dollaford these days. You must have seen in the papers all about that skeleton up to the farm bricked up in a chimney. Somebody must've put it there.'

Pollard made a gesture of recollection.

'Of course. The name's been ringing a bell in my head. Do any of the family live there now, Mrs . . .?'

'Mrs Barratt, sir. You could say Mr Paul Anstey does, in a manner of speaking. He's a rich businessman up in London and comes down for a night or two in and out. 'Twould make better sense to sell the place, but 'tis said he can't because of his father's Will. If Paul dies without a lawful son seems that the farm goes to Hugh, his younger brother, and seeing Hugh's dead, 'twill go to Martin, Mr John's grandson. And he's a very nice young fellow. He was down here in Dollaford weekend before this, trying to get in touch with his uncle, but Paul wasn't up at the farm, wherever he was.'

Pollard had little difficulty in keeping the conversation

87

on the iniquities of Paul Anstey, and in particular how he had gone off from the job his father had found him in London way back before the war and never come home or sent his Dad a line. But in Mrs Barratt's eyes the last straw had been Paul's failure to attend Mr John's funeral. The village had been wild about it, and saw to it that the flowers were lovely, for all that it was December and they cost a fortune.

'Mind you, sir,' she went on, 'I wouldn't like to go into the witness box and say on oath Paul *wasn't* there, all togged up so as nobody'd recognise him after twenty-five years. Not seeing what happened that night, I wouldn't. My hubby's sexton here, and we came over early next morning just to see everything was nice, and we couldn't believe our eyes. The wreaths was thrown all over the place and trampled on.'

Pollard expressed suitable astonishment and horror.

'Kids?' he queried. 'A gang running wild?'

Mrs Barratt was emphatic that twenty and more years back there hadn't been a child in Dollaford that would have even thought of doing such a thing.

'No more there would be now,' she asserted stoutly. 'I don't say we're all plaster saints, but we're decent folk here in Dollaford.'

Pollard detected approaching footsteps in the churchyard as he assured Mrs Barratt that he fully accepted her estimate of the local population. He became repetitive, wondering what was holding Toye up in the porch. At last the south door opened and the latter appeared. Pollard performed introductions and drew Toye's attention to features of interest in the church and its high standard of maintenance. Finally the two men took their leave. They drove out for a short distance on the Polharbour road and parked in a lay-by.

'What's up your sleeve?' Pollard asked.

Toye embarked on a characteristically ordered statement of his reconnaisance.

'There's a fair-sized car park behind the pub,' he said. 'It's overlooked by the windows at the back: kitchen premises and what I took to be back bedrooms on the first floor. You get to the park by way of a narrow unsurfaced lane by the side of the house. I strolled up it, and after about a hundred and fifty yards it ended in a field gate giving on to rough grass sloping up to Sinneldon.'

'Any houses on the right hand side of this lane as you go up to the gate?'

'There's a small cottage right at the junction with the main road. A smallish garden behind it, very nicely kept with one of those old well heads and a wooden shed big enough to take a small car, and a gate giving on the lane. I couldn't check on the car as the shed doors were shut.'

'Disappointing for a chap with a car fixation like yours,' Pollard commented. 'I suppose both the pub and this cottage have back doors?'

'That's right. Both of 'em.'

'Suggestive,' Pollard said thoughtfully. 'Handy unobtrusive short cut to Anstey's Farm for the chap who landed up in the chimney? Also for last week's arsonist? I wonder. While you and Parkin were up on the top just now I was chewing over the idea that somebody local might have some obsessive grievance against the Anstey family. The churchyard business was a whack at old John. Had he been getting abusive letters and threats during his lifetime? We don't know and it's highly unlikely that we ever shall. Last Saturday night somebody tried to burn down the farm. On the face of it this looks like an attack on Paul. However, Mrs Barratt knew about the reversion of the property to Hugh and Hugh's son, so quite possibly other local people know about it, too. The anonymous letter to Highcastle about Martin Anstey's car was obviously an attempt to get him involved in the arson enquiry. But of course the weak point in this vendetta hypothesis is the long interval between John's funeral and the arson. That is, unless there have been anti-Paul activities since he inherited the farm which he's kept to himself for some reason. That's something we'd better try to get out of him when he turns up. If he does.'

'Of course there was that dancing bloke,' Toye took up. 'He sounds a bit wanting to my mind. If he's of an age to have done the churchyard job – in his forties now, say – there mayn't be any rational motive behind the arson or the letter.'

Pollard groaned.

'Only too true. One just clutches at straws in this bloody case. All we can do is plough on, and as the skeleton's our job and it was found on Paul's property we'd better concentrate on him to start with. Tomorrow's hopeless for grilling the locals. Village life will be focused on Sunday dinner and sleeping it off. Unless we hear from the Yard that Paul has turned up unexpectedly or arrives tomorrow, I think it's worth calling on the owner of the kennels where his dog is parked. *Dogdays* it's called. We'll find out from the Highcastle chaps where the place is. Meanwhile I'm for one of the Southgate steaks and an early night. This day seems to have been going on for ever.'

Toye concurred and switched on the ignition. As they drove through Dollaford the sight of the church jogged Pollard's memory.

'What held you up in the church porch?' he asked. 'I thought you were never coming to rescue me from Mrs Barratt?'

'The list of electors. I had a look to see who lives in that cottage on the other side of the lane from the pub.'

'One up to you, old man. I'm not as familiar with church

90

porches as you are, I regret to say. Anyway, who does live in it?'

Somebody called Venner, Joan. There can't be anybody else entitled to a vote. Maybe she's a widow.'

'Going back to what we were thinking about that lane being a short cut to Anstey's Farm,' Pollard said as they left Dollaford behind, 'we'll get Highcastle to collect up some gen on Venner, Joan. Also on the landlord of the Peatcutters. Hooper, the name is, isn't it? It isn't as though there's all that much grist to our mill at the moment.'

Chapter 8

The next morning Pollard and Toye called in at Highcastle police headquarters to pinpoint *Dogdays* on a largescale map of the district. They located it at a short distance off the Sinnel valley road at about two miles beyond Dollaford. In the room allotted to them as a temporary office a copy of a report from the FBI was waiting for them. Paul Anstey, who was being kept under unobtrusive observation, had booked his flight to London for the following Tuesday.

'Could be a blind, of course,' Pollard commented. 'They seem to be doing their stuff over there, anyway. Let's go, shall we?'

The Rover was soon on the now familiar road which branched off the main route linking Highcastle with Polharbour, just outside the city. There had been light overnight rain but this had now cleared, leaving a misty pale blue sky. Pollard let down his window and inhaled gulps of fragrant hay-scented air. Born and bred in the country he often envied his younger brother who was farming successfully in Sussex, and wondered why he himself had embarked on a career which was bound to involve a high proportion of urban life. He would retire to the country of course. He and Jane were absolutely at one on this idea. And the fact that their twin son Andrew, now aged thirteen, had been announcing his intention of becoming a farmer for the past three years secretly delighted them. Unwise to press the idea, of course, while at the same time essential to get it across that top agricultural colleges demanded decent A levels from would-be entrants these days.

Some haymaking was still going on in the fields they passed and Pollard embarked on an argument with Toye, always severely practical, on the relative merits of the old-fashioned picturesque haycock and the contemporary rectangular block of cut hay. They passed through Affacombe with the mass of Sinneldon beginning to loom impressively on their right, and reached the approach to Anstey's Farm. A group of hikers was disappearing up the track. Ghouls, he thought, and then reflected that he was possibly being unfair. They could quite well be nice healthy-minded types out for a day on the moor. Dollaford's main street was almost deserted. A number of cars parked outside the church indicated a Sunday morning service in progress. A few more minutes brought a noticeboard in sight at the entrance to a lane on the right hand side of the road. They slowed down to read it. In black lettering on a white ground it announced.

DOGDAYS
A DOG'S HOTEL
ACCOMMODATION. SKILLED AND LOVING CARE
M. Pettinger.   Tel: Dollaford 432

Toye snorted and turned cautiously down the lane. Its hedges were laced with honeysuckle, and it ended at a white cottage the door of which stood half open. There were various outbuildings dotted about. As the car advanced an indescribable tumult of barking, howling, yelping and yapping broke out behind the cottage. As Pollard wondered how he was going to converse with M. Pettinger a woman in a white overall emerged from the door and came up to his window, cupping her mouth with her hands.

'They'll quieten down if you'll just switch off,' she managed to make him hear. 'You see they don't recognise your engine.'

Toye switched off and the uproar promptly began to subside.

'Miss Pettinger?' Pollard enquired politely.

'Miss Mabel Pettinger, proprietor of *Dogdays*. You've come to make enquiries and see over the kennels, I expect?'

'To make enquiries, yes,' he told her, 'but not the sort of enquiries you usually get, I'm afraid. Here's my official card, and this is my assistant, Inspector Toye, also of Scotland Yard. You may have heard that I'm in charge of the enquiry into the death of the man whose skeleton has been found at Anstey's Farm near here.'

As she studied the card he placed her in her fifties. Her bobbed hair was greying and her pleasant face weatherbeaten. Capable, he thought, but her IQ only average. She looked at him with a puzzled expression.

'What in the world makes you think that *Dogdays* has anything to do with this dreadful business at the farm?' she asked.

'I've no reason whatever to think it has, Miss Pettinger,' he assured her, 'but *Dogdays* being where it is, it's just possible that you may be able to give us some information we'd be glad to have.'

'Well, come inside and sit down, and I'll gladly answer any questions I can, but I can't see how it's going to help you.'

94

She led the way towards the cottage. A door on the right of a narrow flagged passage opened on to a living room. It was simply but attractively furnished in traditional cottage style with flowered chintz chair covers and curtains and good china in alcoves on either side of the fireplace. But its most noticeable feature was the photographs of dogs which lined the walls. The dogs were of varied breeds and often accompanied by humans with the gratified and doting expressions of proud owners. To build up a friendly atmosphere, Pollard expressed interest.

'Some of your clients, I expect?' he asked, indicating the display.

Mabel Pettinger beamed at him.

'That's right. And there are a lot more going up the stairs and some special ones in my bedroom. Sit down, shall we?' She folded her hands in her lap and looked at Pollard with a kind of puzzled expectancy.

From his early days in the CID he had discovered that for him the most productive approach when questioning a potential witness was one emerging from his subconscious on the spur of the moment. This technique baffled Toye who was by nature a careful planner, but he was obliged to admit its almost invariable effectiveness.

'Would you say, Miss Pettinger,' he began almost casually, 'that people round here dislike the Anstey family?'

He observed a surprised reaction to this question, and noted small red patches come up below her cheekbones. What had put her on the defensive, he wondered?

'Of course they've been here a lot longer than I have,' she said. 'Old John Anstey was still alive when I bought this place. I've heard some of the old folk say he'd been a hard man in his time, but most seemed sorry for him living out at the farm on his own, with his wife dead and his sons gone off. But somebody had it in for him. A shameful thing happened after he was buried.'

'You mean,' Pollard asked, 'what was done to his grave?'

'That's right. And they never got to the bottom of it. People still talk about it.'

'Well, what about his son Paul who inherited the farm? You board his dog, I think, so I expect you see something of him? Is he unpopular with the locals?'

There was a brief pause. Pollard watched the red patches deepen.

'Well, I suppose he is with some of them,' Mabel Pettinger admitted reluctantly. 'They're a funny lot, the Dollaford village people. Set in their ways over some things. It's held against Paul that he didn't come down to his father's funeral, though how he was to know of it I can't tell you. Paul isn't one to talk about himself, but from odd things he's said, it seems that his father put him into a job in London when he left school. Paul didn't like it and went off to make his own way. Never wrote or came back on a visit. It was wrong of him, I'll grant you, but seeing what the old people say about John Anstey, I don't doubt that there were faults on both sides. And I'll tell you this,' she went on, her voice rising slightly as she looked Pollard straight in the face, 'I've never had to do with a better client or a nicer gentleman than Paul Anstey. A real dog-lover he is.'

Pollard listened to a glowing account of Paul Anstey's rescue of a puppy thrown out of a car by heartless people to fend for itself. Paul had been driving down to the farm and brought the puppy straight to *Dogdays* where it had remained ever since with the status of a parlour boarder. A banker's order covered its maintenance, and every year Paul raised the amount to keep up with inflation. When he came down to the farm he always dropped in to see how Cerby was doing.

'Cerby?' Pollard queried. 'That's an unusual name.'

Mabel Pettinger explained that it was short for some Latin name that she just couldn't call to mind.

'Cerberus?' he suggested.

'That's it. A dog in a story ugly enough to frighten you, Paul said. It was just his joke, of course. But you've got to admit dear Cerby's no beauty. Here he is,' she went on, getting up to unhook photographs from the wall, 'and here he is with his master.'

Pollard hastily registered a portrait of an unusual compound of bulldog head, jowl and front legs and a feathery King Charles spaniel hindquarters. He passed it over to an impassive Toye, and concentrated on the second photograph in which Cerby sat at the feet of a man on a garden bench dressed in good tweeds and with an amused, slightly challenging face. Sixtyish, he thought, memorising the man's features.

'Cerby mayn't be in line for a first at Crufts,' he said, handing the portrait to Toye, 'but he looks highly intelligent and very friendly.'

'He's a love,' Mabel Pettinger agreed enthusiastically. 'The staff make quite a silly of him. Especially Brian Moss.'

'Do you find it difficult to get staff?' Pollard asked.

'Not as a rule. Sometimes when we're full right up I could do with a bit extra. I've got a couple of first-rate girls who come up from the village and Brian's resident. I've rigged up a little flat for him over the old stable. I was lucky to find him, and he's lucky to have landed up here. He went to a special school and couldn't cope with a factory job or anything like that, but he's simply wonderful with animals – like St Francis of Assisi, you know. Good with his hands, too. And now he's got a girlfriend, and they're getting married in August. I'm enlarging the flat for them. Such a nice motherly type, the daughter of a

97

farm labourer. She' – Mabel Pettinger broke off and listened. 'Yes, there's the midday walk coming back with Brian. Come out and meet him and Cerby. Cerby goes on all the walks, running free.'

Pollard's immediate reaction to Brian Moss was that in appearance he was totally unlike the Little Poor Man of Assisi as portrayed by Italian artists. A six-footer, he was dark, thin and loose-limbed to the point of being ungainly as he moved.

Quite suddenly a thought took shape in Pollard's mind as he listened to the young man's shy responses to Mabel Pettinger's attempts to draw him into conversation. Cerby at Brian's side licked his hand while wagging his preposterous plumed tail.

'They're such buddies, these two,' she said. 'Last time Mr Paul Anstey was here he said that if he ever had to give up coming down to the farm he'd give Cerby to Brian for keeps. . . . Oh dear, there's the phone. Just show these gentlemen round the kennels, Brian, and then you must go off for your half-day: it's nearly twelve. I won't be more than a few minutes.'

Escorted by Brian they inspected the other dogs in residence, each with its kennel equipped with central heating and a spacious run enclosed in wire netting.

'I wonder if Mr Anstey will rebuild the farm?' Pollard remarked casually, glancing up in time to catch a satisfied secretive smile on Brian's face. 'Have you seen the place since the fire?'

'Yes, I've seen it. Not worth rebuildin', I'd say.'

'My wife and I walked along the Sinneldon track the day before the fire, as it happens. You get a good view of the farm looking down from the top, don't you?'

He sensed a sudden, almost instinctive caution.

'I dunno. . . . Here's Miss Pettinger back. I'd better be off to me girl's fer me Sunday dinner. . . . Cerby: stay!'

He ambled off at a fair speed, swinging his long arms and anxiously watched by the dog which gave a little whimper.

'Where does his girl live?' Pollard asked Mabel Pettinger.

'Her father's got a cottage on a hill farm up on the moor. You follow the Sinneldon track up there for about a couple of miles, beyond the Anstey's Farm combe, and then strike off to the left.'

As they made their way back to the Rover parked in front of the cottage, Pollard paused to look at the group of outbuildings. A ladder was propped against one of the more distant ones with various building materials on the ground beside it.

'That's where you're enlarging Brian's flat, I expect?'

'Yes. Adding on a couple of rooms and smartening the place up a bit. Brian's doing the redecorating in his off time. . . . Well, I don't feel I've had much to tell you, Mr Pollard: Superintendent Pollard, perhaps I ought to call you.'

'Perhaps you've told us more than you think, Miss Pettinger,' he replied. 'Just one last routine question and then we'll remove ourselves. The fire at Anstey's Farm was started deliberately some time during the night of Saturday, June the sixteenth. That's a week ago last night. You don't, I suppose, remember seeing or hearing any stranger about at any time over that weekend? Or a car starting up in your lane?'

'Nothing out of the ordinary that I can call to mind,' she replied decisively. 'Anyway it would have set off the dogs good and proper. They know a strange step as well as a strange car like yours just now.'

'I could do with a drink, couldn't you?' Pollard remarked as Toye braked at the junction of the lane with the main road. 'Not the Peatcutters though, at this hour on a Sunday morning. We'd better head for the Southgate and have a decent Sunday lunch as well. What price Brian as the bloke the fireman saw leaping about early last Monday morning? Of course the 64,000-dollar question is whether he was feeling exhilarated at the result of his efforts in the arson line during the Saturday night. At least we've got a possible lead of a negative sort out of this interview.'

'Would you say he's round the bend?' Toye asked, emerging on to the main road.

'No. I don't think it's as simple as that. There was a lad rather like him in my home village. The people said he was a "natural", and looking back I can see they meant somebody who knew things more by instinct than by the usual way of learning about them and reasoning. Brian seems to have instinctive understanding of animals, and how to manipulate things with his hands in the sort of simple jobs Miss Pettinger would want done at *Dogdays*. He's obviously hooked on Cerby, and would be able to take in Paul Anstey's remark about handing him over if he – Paul, I mean – ever gave up the farm and stopped coming down to these parts. I can imagine Brian's mind working something like this. . . . If Anstey's Farm wasn't there, Paul wouldn't come any more, and he'd give me Cerby. . . . If I set fire to it one night it wouldn't be there any more. . . . He'd miss out completely on any other outcome of burning the place down. Absolute singlemindedness, in fact.'

They drove on in silence. Finally Toye announced that he could see the idea, but what about the practical possibilities? Could he have slipped out of *Dogdays* and got back again on two consecutive nights without rousing the dogs?

'Don't overlook the point that Brian's flat is well away

from the cottage and the kennel area. And if it's true that the dogs only raise hell at unfamiliar sounds, they wouldn't have barked at hearing him about at unusual times. Well, I suppose we'll have to follow it up, perhaps by directly challenging Brian in front of the Pettinger woman. It would be something to eliminate the arson from the list of attacks on the Ansteys for being Ansteys.'

Despite the fact that it was midsummer the Southgate laid on a traditional Sunday lunch of roast beef, Yorkshire pudding and apple pie with clotted cream. Pollard and Toye attacked it with the zest of men uncertain of when their next meal will materialise, and having done it full justice they retired to the hotel lounge to read the Sunday papers over coffee.

'Excuse me, sir.' Pollard surfaced with a start over an hour later to find one of the Southgate's receptionists beside his chair. 'You're wanted on the telephone: Inspector Parkin speaking from the police station.'

'Thanks.' Pollard struggled to his feet with a wink at Toye and followed her out of the room.

He was absent for so long that Toye looked up enquiringly when he eventually reappeared.

'A small step forward,' Pollard told him. 'Brian Moss is out as far as the fire at Anstey's Farm goes. It's Highcastle's concern primarily, of course, as they're in charge of the arson enquiry and they're jolly grateful, but we're saved from wasting any time on Brian and his antics. Remember how he clammed up and made off when my interest in what you could see of the house from the edge of the combe got a bit near the bone? His girlfriend and future wife is called Rosaleen Tucker, and her father works at Highhays, a big hill farm up on Crownmoor. She may be a nice motherly type as the Pettinger said. Obviously Brian appeals to her maternal instinct, and just let anybody look like being a threat to him and she goes

101

over the top. He seems to have rushed to her for protection from the London cops who were trying to make out he'd set the farm on fire. Wasting not a moment, Rosaleen leapt on to her moped, headed for the nearest telephone box, dialled police HQ, and demanded to be put through to the boss man. Poor old Parkin is on duty today and got it full blast. She says that Brian was at Gorse Cottage where she lives with her parents from after lunch on the Saturday to about half-past four on the Sunday morning. No prizes are offered for guessing where and with whom he was from bedtime onwards.'

'Disgraceful, I call it,' Toye commented austerely. 'And it's no alibi that I can see. Only the girl's word for it.'

'Rosaleen's father and mother are prepared to swear in any court of law, they say, that the pair spent the night in Rosaleen's bedroom. It's a small cottage: two rooms up and two down, and they were in the other bedroom themselves. Their attitude is robust. Mr Tucker remarked that anyway Brian and Rosaleen were getting spliced next August, and he reminded his wife with a guffaw that people had pulled their legs when Rosie was born, saying she was a ruddy fine specimen for a seven-months child.'

After further unfavourable comment on the Tucker family, Toye asked if Brian had admitted being the chap Fireman Forches had seen going on like a lunatic up on the edge of the combe early on the Monday morning.

'Yes, he's quite open about it. He says that on the way back from Gorse Cottage he first of all smelt smoke and then he saw it rising up from the combe. He ran to the edge and looked down and there was Anstey's Farm burning merrily. He reacted just as I said he would. The place would be burnt down, and Paul wouldn't have anywhere to come to and would give him Cerby. With a mentality like his no other aspect of the situation would occur to

102

him. So he did nothing about raising the alarm. Just went back to *Dogdays*, let himself quietly into his flat and started on the first jobs of the day at the usual time. Only he was feeling so exhilarated about the future that he couldn't resist going along for another gloat early on the Monday morning. When he felt it was time to start for home again he says he felt so good that he jumped in the air a bit. Then a chap down below shouted up at him and he scarpered for *Dogdays* for all he was worth.'

A meditative silence descended, ultimately broken by Toye.

'Well, since Moss is out and Highcastle still haven't come up with any vandals on the loose during the Saturday night of the fire, isn't it coming round again to look as though somebody's definitely got it in for the Ansteys?' he said.

Pollard leant back in his chair and clasped his hands behind his head.

'I'm beginning to wonder if the situation won't turn out to be more complicated that that, you know,' he said. 'It's the time factor that's so baffling. Let's recap, beginning with old John Anstey. He died suddenly in his bed from a certifiable disease nearly twenty-five years ago. According to his doctor's report he was physically fit up to his death and could have murdered a chap and stowed the corpse in the chimney. Paul cannot be located, so John's burial takes place in Dollaford churchyard, and on the night after the funeral somebody chucks the wreaths all over the place. Mrs Barratt hinted to me darkly that Paul might have been at the funeral and responsible for the vandalism, but this idea seems to be a bit far-fetched, don't you think?'

Toye agreed, on the grounds that it would have been a daft risk to take if you meant to avoid being run to earth for the next couple of months. Mightn't it be a mistake to

103

attach any importance to the wreaths business? John Anstey seemed to have been a ruthless old tough and might well have got across somebody in Dollaford who'd nursed a grievance against him for years?'

'I've come to that conclusion myself,' Pollard said. 'Let's put the bloody wreath business into cold storage *pro tem* and move on to a possible local vendetta against Paul. He's the Mystery Man in this case. Apart from his war service, what was he doing from the time he walked out of the job his father found for him in the early 1930s to his reappearance as a bloke sufficiently sure of himself to take the risk of launching a travel agency in February 1961? I only hope that the chaps I put on to ferret out his private life are getting hold of some useful information. Anyway, he could have committed murder and stowed away the corpse while living alone at the farm for a time after he reappeared. Admittedly local people don't seem very keen on him except for the Pettinger, but so far as we know he hasn't been the target of any open hostility between 1961 and the arson a week ago yesterday. What suddenly sparked off anti-Ansteyism, if that's what it was?'

'It looks as though Martin Anstey's turning up out of the blue must have had something to do with it, especially as somebody tried to pin the arson on him,' Toye said tenaciously.

'Yes, but what, for heaven's sake? It couldn't surely have been personal hostility to him as we've said before, because of his past history, so I suppose that anonymous letter could be pure anti-Ansteyism. Or it might simply have been sent by some bloody-minded motorist who'd been obstructed by the Maestro in the Peatcutters' car park. It's extraordinary how rabid people can get where their cars are concerned. . . . Here, let's switch off and ring for some tea. I think this ghastly case is one of the worst snarl-ups we've ever had pushed on to us.'

104

On returning from a tour of Highcastle on foot, Pollard encountered Toye who had opted for an inspection of the Cathedral.

'Well, anyway,' he said, 'I've a credible plan of campaign for tomorrow. We'll start by throwing our weight about over getting an early appointment with John Anstey's solicitors. Paul may employ them too on business connected with the farm. We'll then return to the Yard, see what gen has been collected for us, and then snatch a night at home. Tuesday is an unknown quantity at the moment, apart from the fact that Paul Anstey is alleged to be flying in at some point.'

Toye expressed unqualified satisfaction and they headed for the bar.

Chapter 9

At nine o'clock on the following morning, Pollard rang Messrs Hepplewhite, Neale and Royland, the Highcastle solicitors who had acted for John Anstey, and after his death for Paul in matters connected with the farm. He made effective use of his rank in the CID, and was immediately offered an appointment for ten o'clock with Mr Hepplewhite, the senior partner.

The firm occupied two adjoining houses in one of the city's finest Georgian crescents. Grumbling at having no time to inspect their elegant frontages of rose-red brick, Pollard led the way through an eighteenth-century doorway into the reception area. He learnt that Mr Hepplewhite would see him at once, and accompanied by Toye was escorted to a spacious room on the first floor. A man in late middle age, grey-haired and with observant grey eyes got up from his desk to greet them. As they shook hands Pollard apologised for having disrupted the morning's scheduled programme.

'Please don't apologise,' Mr Hepplewhite said, indicating two chairs drawn up to face him across the desk. 'In the first place I'm delighted to have the opportunity of meeting you, Chief Superintendent. And I'm sure I needn't tell you that all Highcastle is agog at the happenings over at Anstey's Farm, and I shall dine out on this meeting for months. What can I do for you?'

'It's a matter of delving into past history,' Pollard told him. 'The forensic scientists are satisfied that the skeleton found in the chimney at the farm is that of a man who was murdered between twenty and thirty years ago. Analysis of the brickwork blocking off the chimney confirms this, so the vital period is the ten years between 1954 and 1964. We want to find out everything we possibly can about what was going on at the farm during this period. As the Ansteys' solicitors, have you any records of the place having been let, for instance, or of any trouble there? Is there anyone either still in practice in this firm or available who could produce any information that might help our enquiry into the murder?'

Mr Hepplewhite pursed his lips and gave a little shrug of his shoulders.'

'It's most unfortunate,' he said, 'but Peter Royland, who had handled the Ansteys' affairs from about 1936 onwards died three years ago. The only thing I can suggest is that you have a talk with his son David who joined us as a junior partner in 1978. We're rather specialised these days, but try to keep personal links with long-standing family clients, and David took over the Ansteys from his father. Peter had a long illness – it was cancer, poor chap – and I know he spent a lot of time discussing the work with David. Would you like to see him?'

'We certainly should,' Pollard replied.

After a short interval David Royland became available. A young man in his early thirties, he was informal in dress and speech in comparison with the senior partner, and his room was smaller and slightly untidy, but he impressed Pollard from the start as intelligent and perceptive.

'I'm with you,' he said, after listening to a brief résumé

107

of the significance of the period 1954 to 1964. 'Of course the old boy – John Anstey – was before my time as far as your investigation goes. But my father looked after his affairs from just before the Second World War until John died in 1960. How much do you know, sir, about what one might call the decline and fall of the Anstey family?'

Pollard briefly listed the financial difficulties of the thirties, the death of John Anstey's wife in 1932, the break between Paul and his father, the war service of both Paul and Hugh and the latter's emigration to Southern Rhodesia in 1945.

'You're jolly well genned up on them,' David Royland remarked when the recital came to an end. 'I really don't think I can add much to what you already know.'

'Mr Hepplewhite told us just now that your father briefed you on any clients you would be taking on from him,' Pollard replied. 'On the strength of the forensic scientists' reports on the skeleton we're concentrating on the years 1954 to 1964. Anything you can pass on about John Anstey's later life could be relevant. And in general, what sort of chap was he?'

David Royland grinned.

'Not the easiest of clients, according to Dad. Disgruntled at his much reduced income and always harping back to the good old days. He was on pretty short commons, although it seems that Hugh, the younger son, helped out. Dad was simply staggered when John made a Will leaving a life interest in what remained of the property to Paul, who'd simply faded out in the middle '30s and vanished without trace. Apparently he – John – had a thing about the family home going to the eldest son, anyway in the first instance. Still thought of himself as a landed proprietor, apparently.'

'Was there any trouble with locals during the latter part of his life?' Pollard asked.

'Nothing that got as far as this firm, anyway. Going back a good bit further, though, he was paying out £100 per annum in quarterly instalments to a London solicitor from 1917 to 1931. When I took over Dad's remaining clients I found the receipts at the bottom of the Anstey deeds box.'

There was a brief charged silence. Pollard's and David Royland's eyes met and Toye suspended his note taking.

'Fourteen years,' Pollard commented. 'The school leaving age was fourteen in those days, wasn't it?'

'This is it,' David Royland replied. 'Maintenance payments, don't you think? Difficult but not impossible to trace. You'd like the receipts, I expect?'

'Please. We'll give you an official receipt for them. A kid born in 1917 would have been thirty-seven in 1954. . . . The forensic report dates the skeleton as that of a man between thirty-five and forty-five. There may possibly be a link-up here. Anyway, Mr Royland, many thanks for this bit of info. May we go on to Paul Anstey now? I understand that your father had the job of tracking him down after John Anstey's death?'

'That's right. He was eventually run to earth organising skiing holidays in Switzerland in February 1961. He told Dad that after being demobbed he'd tried various jobs and come to the conclusion that tourism was going to be the money spinner of the future, and got into it in the first place by working for tourist set-ups abroad. I think he eventually started up on his own in the early '60s. Anyway, he's made a good thing of it.'

'I suppose your father saw something of him over John Anstey's Will?'

'Yes, he did, and I remember him telling me that Paul looked younger than he expected, and struck him as an able tough with a reckless streak, and that Hugh's interests would need watching. Since I took over he hasn't made much use of us down here, except for a few odd things about the farm. I imagine his travel firm has a London solicitor.'

'Any trouble with the locals after he turned up?'

'None, as far as I know. Is he still out of the country?'

'We have been informed that he's flying back to London tomorrow. I expect he'll be along about the insurance situation and what the legal position is over rebuilding. Hugh's son Martin is now living permanently in the UK, and as the property reverts to him on Paul's death, I foresee quite a job for you people here. Incidentally he's tried but failed to make contact with Paul.'

David Royland grinned again. 'I straight dream on fees,' he said, 'Believe it or not, we put on *Romeo and Juliet* at school. Juliet was borrowed from a girl's establishment not far off and was she not a smasher?'

'Beware,' Pollard riposted, 'of "the fair round belly". We put on *As You Like It*.'

They parted on the best of terms and an undertaking to keep in touch over future developments in the enquiry. Walking to the car park Toye remarked that he had read *The Merchant of Venice* but had not been able to make much of it.

'Funny sort of legal system they had,' he commented. 'Not really what you'd call a system to my mind.'

'Home James, and don't spare the horses,' Pollard said as they emerged into the street. 'At least we've got a remotely possible lead on the bloody skeleton now.'

As soon as he arrived at the Yard Pollard contacted Hildebrand Robinson, a former brilliant and definitely eccentric classics master at a leading public school for boys. On learning that the governors had decided to admit girls to the sixth forms he had promptly sent in his resignation. All attempts to persuade him to withdraw it

110

failed. He was rapidly inundated with offers of interesting jobs involving above average intelligence, one being research into various types of records on behalf of Scotland Yard.

'Well, what's up this time?' he demanded in response to the telephone call from Pollard. 'Anything to do with that male skeleton affair you're alleged to be investigating?'

'Correct,' Pollard replied. 'We're interested in a bloke called John Anstey who owned the farmhouse where the skeleton has turned up. He died in 1960, aged 70. Between 1917 and 1931 he was paying out £100 per annum to a firm of Holborn solicitors, Brown and Haycroft. It suggests to us a possible maintenance payment for a by-blow, up to the school-leaving age of that period. The forensics are prepared to state that in their considered opinion the owner of the skeleton had his head smashed in at some point during the decade 1954 to 1964. We're virtually clueless at the moment and think it's worth investigating the by-blow possibility, especially if the end product was a boy. He – if he ever existed – would have been fortyish at the end of the 1950s, and in theory might have turned up with blackmail in mind. OK so far?'

'Clear as daylight. I suppose you want me to go along to St Catherine's House and plough through the birth certificates of the period.'

'Just that. And having tracked down the little chap, we'll be raring to know if he was adopted, and who by but our chaps can ferret that out.'

'Always assuming that it was a legal adoption, and that as solicitors were involved, it seems likely, it shouldn't be beyond their powers. Is this job urgent? My talents are greatly in demand just now, I'd have you know.'

111

'Vitally urgent,' Pollard assured him. 'It's one hell of a case and hotting up.'

'So be it,' Hildebrand Robinson replied oracularly and rang off.

Pollard laughed as he replaced the receiver, and went off to the appointment that he had asked for with his Assistant Commissioner. Over the years of working together their relationship had become more relaxed.

'I grant you this case is a bit of a snorter,' the AC commented when Pollard's résumé of developments up to date came to its end. 'All the same, there are one or two redeeming features, though. The forensic chaps have agreed on the period of the murder which narrows your field. Pity it takes in both father and son. In my opinion it's a sound move to get old Hildebrand on the trail of a possible illegitimate son of John's. If there was one he'll track him down, and any subsequent adoption, too. He's a bloodhound when he's on the trail of specific facts.'

In a further discussion they agreed that various points made a theory of such a son turning up at Anstey's Farm possibly with blackmail in mind a reasonable suggestion. Born in 1917 when the payments of the London solicitor began, he would have been 40 in 1957. At this stage his father was 67, and according to his doctor, in excellent health. So the murder and the subsequent bricking up of the corpse in the chimney would have been a physical possibility. Even in summer, when Sinneldon was frequented by hikers and birdwatchers, the farm was isolated.

'Granted all that,' Pollard said, 'I still think Paul Anstey is the better bet, assuming a suitable victim.'

The AC agreed.

'You're not suddenly up to the neck in drug trafficking,' he said. 'The suggestion is that he's been a wrong 'un for some time. Those chunks of his life when he was completely off stage want looking into. And his army record. You'll want extra help, I suppose?'

'Well, yes sir. There's a good deal of ground to cover. Marlchester may have records of what their Old Boys did on leaving. We know Paul walked out of the insurance office job his father found for him. Or was he kicked out? Then there's his army record as you say.'

'You needn't go into any further detail,' the AC cut in gloomily. 'You've got Toye and I suppose you'd better have a couple more suitable chaps to help in making all those investigations. . . . What about the young Anstey? Paul's nephew? Obviously he couldn't have been involved in the murder, but does he know anything?'

'I'm prepared to write him off at any rate *pro tem*, sir. Very satisfactory reports on him from South Africa, and he's very frank on his family history.'

The two men sat in silence for a short space.

'Suppose Paul Anstey vanishes into thin air overnight instead of turning up at Heathrow?' Pollard propounded.

'Over to Interpol, and another job for you in the meantime,' the AC replied robustly. 'Well, I don't see that we can do anything more at the moment. Keep me posted. It's an intriguing case.'

Pollard went back to his own office and in consultation with Toye contacted Detective-Sergeants Longman and Chandler, both of whom had carried out useful investigations for him in some of his previous cases. The Anstey's Farm murder was discussed at length and the various fields of enquiry allotted.

'No action to be taken, of course, until I've seen Anstey,' Pollard said.

As he spoke his desk telephone bleeped and he picked up the receiver. As he listened his colleagues saw his eyebrows go up and a sudden vitalisation of his face.

'Anstey's airborne,' he told them at the end of the call.

'Due at Heathrow at 23.30 GMT. He'll be under obbo from touchdown onwards, of course.'

Excitement was running high in the Pollard home at Wimbledon. Tickets and hotel reservation vouchers had arrived for the fortnight in Switzerland which was to be the thirteen-year-old twins' first experience of foreign travel. Jane had picked up a fresh batch of brochures in a branch of Thomas Cook's and the prospect of soaring skywards in a chair lift was almost excessively exhilarating. Finally she insisted on a belated bedtime and peace descended on the sitting room.

Coffee was sipped in virtual silence.

'I suppose the press has gone to town?' Pollard asked as he set down an empty cup for the second time.

Jane indicated a pile of newspapers on a side table in the window.

'I've read every word while you've been down there. Could you face an offical recap or are you too flat out?'

'It would help,' Pollard replied. 'But I warn you that there's a lot of it. Stop me when you can't take any more.'

'I'm hooked. Don't forget that I know the geographical background, and those snippets of information we had from Olivia about the Ansteys. . . .'

There was a lengthy silence when his summary of developments up to date came to an end.

'At first sight a neat local affair,' Jane said at last, 'and then one begins to see the snags. The skeleton can't possibly be a local's. People don't disappear unnoticed from places like the Sinnel valley.'

'Granted,' Pollard replied. 'Even casual strangers are noticed and discussed. Of course a walker following our route could have dropped down into the combe and been bumped off by either John or Paul, but the chap would have come from somewhere and there would have been enquiries locally. Then there are the three things which could indicate anti-Anstey feeling. The vandalising of John's grave, the arson and the attempt to implicate Martin. And whoever tried on the last of these must have been around in Dollaford that Saturday night to know that he'd turned up out of the blue, and what his car number was.'

'There's such an extraordinarily long gap, though, between the grave business and the other two things. Nearly twenty-five years. What could have sparked off a hate campaign after all that time? Young Martin's appearance? If so, how come, considering his past history?'

Pollard clasped his hands behind his head and sat frowning.

'I was thinking along that line on the way up today. The only answer seems to be that things *were* going on during those years that we haven't got on to yet. I'm going to put the locals through a sieve as soon as I can get back to Dollaford. The immediate job is putting Paul through one tomorrow morning, of course.'

As he spoke the carriage clock on the mantelpiece chimed the half-hour. Pollard glanced up at it.

'At this moment – if the plane's on time – he's touching down at Heathrow.'

Jane had already begun to collect the empty coffee cups.

'If you don't touch down a pillow pronto,' she said, 'he'll make rings round you.'

Paul Anstey was shown into Pollard's office at the Yard at ten o'clock on the following morning.

'Morning,' he said curtly in response to being greeted. 'You're in charge of the enquiry into this business down at my farm I was told when I rang in. I couldn't get anything

115

out of the Yank police, but now I've seen some papers. What the bloody hell's behind it? That's what I want to know.'

'So do we, Mr Anstey. Won't you sit down?' Pollard replied equably as Toye drew a chair up the desk. . . . 'This is my colleague Detective-Inspector Toye. Naturally we're hoping that you'll be able to give us some useful information.'

As he talked he registered the appearance of the man who sat facing him. . . . Springy dark hair with a frosting of silver and beginning to recede from the forehead. . . . Well-marked features with deep creases running from the nostrils to the corners of the mouth. . . . A network of fine lines radiating from the challenging light eyes . . . cleanshaven . . . a rather weathered complexion . . . obvious determination and drive . . .

'Haven't you Scotland Yard people found out who the dead chap was?' Paul Anstey demanded.

'No,' Pollard replied. 'A bare skeleton is very uninformative unless it shows some abnormalities. This one doesn't. Details of the dental work done on the teeth are being circulated to dentists throughout the UK but the man may have had treatment abroad, of course. The checking of dental records will take some time. The cause of death has been established beyond doubt. It was a violent blow which shattered the left frontal area of the skull. Scientific tests have also established that the man was between thirty-five and forty-five years old when he was killed and that the murder took place not less than twenty and not more than thirty years ago.'

Pollard watched Paul Anstey make a rapid calculation.

'So you're saying that the chap was done in and bunged into the chimney some time between 1954 and 1964, then?'

'Yes. Tests on the mortar used in the brickwork agree

116

with this finding. So obviously we are making enquiries about who was living at the farm during this period, and hoping that you can help us over this.'

Paul Anstey thrust his chair back a little, crossed his legs and contemplated Pollard.

'I can't tell you a bloody thing about who was living there down to my father's death in November 1960. I haven't any personal knowledge about whether he was, or was not, apart from the fact that he actually died there. Anybody at your level will have discovered by now that I left the place in 1934 and never set foot in it again until February 1961, when I heard from the solicitor – Peter Royland of Highcastle – that I'd been left a life interest in it. When I left home in '34 I broke off all contact with my father and also with my only brother, Hugh. He must have emigrated to Southern Rhodesia. I got a stinker of a letter from him about my responsibility for maintenance of the farm. Obviously he'd expected to get it himself. I didn't answer the letter. For all I know he's dead by now.'

'He is,' Pollard replied. 'He and his wife were both killed in a plane crash in 1982.' Watching Paul's reaction to this information he saw the fleeting discomfort that news of the unexpected death of a contemporary brings, however negligible the relationship has been. 'You didn't answer his son Martin's letter either, did you? The one he wrote to you at the farm about three weeks ago to say that he would call in there on the afternoon of Saturday, June 15th?'

To his surprise, he saw blank astonishment on Paul's face, and reflected that if it were not genuine the man was an accomplished actor capable of reacting at lightning speed.

'What the hell do you mean? I've never had a letter from the boy in my life. I've no idea how old he is, even. Do you mean he's over here? In the UK?'

117

'Martin Anstey is thirty. After his parents' death he decided to return permanently to this country, and is working at Randall's, the publishing house.'

'For God's sake. I must get on to him right away about the bloody farm – what's left of it. We'll have to come to some agreement about rebuilding the place – if it's feasible.'

'I quite understand that you'll want to contact him as soon as possible, Mr Anstey, but as the law's agent my concern is with the murder that took place at the farm, and I need to ask you some further questions.'

'Well, let's get on with them, then. I've got a mountain of the firm's business waiting.'

'Certainly. I understand that you served in the army during the war. When were you demobilised?'

'In '45.'

'Where were you living during the next fourteen years, Mr Anstey?'

'Mainly in European countries patronised by British tourists.'

'Surely,' Pollard pursued, 'during this period you must have been in contact with former friends in the Dollaford area and heard news of your father and what was happening down there?'

'You haven't got the message,' Paul Anstey said curtly. 'When I walked out it was a complete break. Nobody knew my address and nobody heard anything from me. And after the war I'd got my sights on making a new life for myself. I'd saved some pay and had my gratuity, and took off from there.'

There was a short pause during which Pollard took in the expensive-looking casuals and the slightly excessive gold signet ring.

'You appear to have been successful,' he said. 'When did you launch *Going Places*?'

118

'Not until 1963, starting in a pretty small way. It stood out a mile in the 1950s that people were fed up with wartime restrictions and whatever and wanted to let up and enjoy themselves. It seemed to me that the holiday trade was a safe bet for the future and that it would be worth learning the job. I'd always been reasonably good at games and knew some French and German, so I went abroad and got taken on at tourist places in Europe and picked up the essentials of running a travel agency. I was in charge of a winter sports set up in Switzerland when the family solicitor ran me to earth early in 1961, and told me my father had died and left me a life interest in the farm.'

'What were your reactions, Mr Anstey?'

'You could have knocked me for six, of course, seeing we'd been completely out of touch since I cleared off in 1934. I'd saved a bit of cash over the years and suddenly thought I'd like to go and have a look at the old place again. So I fixed things up with a firm the centre belonged to and came back to England. But my God! It was sheer bloody hell when I got to the farm. I drove down from Town and picked up the key from a clerk at the solicitor's office. It was pitch dark when I arrived. Cold as hell, too, and so primitive I couldn't believe it. I managed to get a fire going, and mercifully I'd brought some grub with me. Next morning I woke up to about four feet of snow. Not a hope of getting the car out for the next two days.'

Pollard looked thoughtfully at the lounging figure in front of him, hands thrust into trouser pockets and knees casually crossed.

'Was the house much changed?' he asked.

'Not basically,' Paul Anstey replied. 'It seemed smaller, of course. Depressingly dilapidated. The roof was leaking in several places. Hardly any modernisation had been done. And the fireplace in the room at the end

119

where you found your skeleton had been bricked up, of course.'

'Did the bricking-up look recent?'

'It didn't strike me as particularly new. I remember thinking that my father might have had it done to save himself the trouble of making a fire in the room. There was a paraffin heater there, and I found a couple of drums of the stuff in one of the outhouses.'

'When you were able to get over to Dollaford, did you learn anything at all about who had been living at the farm during the last years of your father's life?'

'Damn all. They'd hardly speak to me. I'd never been forgiven for opting out, and particularly for not turning up for my father's funeral. There were some urgent jobs to be done at the farm like roof repairs, and I wanted some reliable female to keep an eye on the place and do for me when I came down now and again. It seemed hopeless, but in the end the landlord of the pub put me in touch with a woman from Polharbour who was coming to live in Dollaford and do part-time work for him. So I fixed up with her.'

'And her name, Mr Anstey?'

'Venner . . .' Paul Anstey tilted his chair backwards and stared fixedly at Pollard. 'Chief Superintendent, isn't it? How about putting our cards on the table? You'd like to pin this murder on either my father or me, wouldn't you? Well, he's out. Take it from me. He was an aggressive type and quite capable of cracking the skull of a chap who'd got across him. But he'd never have been such a bloody fool as to keep the corpse on the premises. He knew Crownmoor like the back of his hand, including the old mine workings with deep shafts going down below water level. And if I'd reacted to an uninvited caller during one of my flying visits early on by bashing in his head, that's what I should have done with his mortal

120

remains. And as I told you, the bricking-up job had already been done by the time I got here in February '61. And there's also the question of who the bloke was whose disappearance seems to have aroused so little interest.'

'Clearly argued, Mr Anstey,' Pollard replies. 'Who, then, do you suggest was responsible for the bloke's murder?'

'Obviously, surely, somebody who made free of the building between my father's death and my return about seven weeks later.'

'Did you find any signs of a break-in when you first came down?'

'No. I found the back door unbolted, though. It looks as though the cleaner recruited by Hepplewhite and Co. to do a bit of clearing up after the funeral was careless.'

'Was she a Dollaford woman?'

'Yes. She must have seen the clearing up as a job for my father, not for me.'

'And her name?'

'I never knew it. Anyway, it wouldn't help you. She died at the end of January '61, before I turned up.'

Pollard contemplated Paul Anstey in silence.

'And you seriously maintain,' he asked him, 'that it wouldn't have struck the owner of the house when he reappeared that one of the fireplaces had been closed up?'

Paul Anstey met his challenging stare unruffled.

'Circumstances alter cases, don't they?' he replied. 'On the mat inside the front door were a few circulars addressed to John Anstey, Anstey's Farm, Dollaford. There were also two envelopes addressed to The Executor of the late John Anstey deceased. And you can add to that the layer of dust over the whole place and the leaking roof and the general dilapidation. Pretty obvious that whoever had been left the house was in no particular hurry to take it over, and unlikely to register that a fireplace had been bricked in recently. Much less risky from the murderer's point of view, too, than parking a body on the moor which he was unlikely to know at all well.'

'Quite,' Pollard replied urbanely. 'May we have the name of the builders you engaged to do the repairs at the farm?'

'It was a small Polharbour firm. . . . Wait a bit . . . Blount the chap was called. A small set-up, but their work was OK.'

'Got that, Inspector?' Pollard asked Toye. 'Well, Mr Anstey, we needn't detain you much longer. Inspector Toye will just have his shorthand record of this interview transcribed and typed for you to sign. We have your private address and telephone number, and as you're an important witness in this enquiry we must ask you not to leave this country at the moment. Good morning,' he concluded, getting to his feet.

Paul Anstey also got up, returned the greeting ungraciously and was escorted out of the room by Toye.

'Type I can't do with,' Toye remarked on his return holding a sheet of typescript by one corner and putting it into the file. 'Take him down a peg, wouldn't it, if he knew Drugs were waiting outside to latch on to him?'

'Of course he could have done the skeleton job,' Pollard said without looking up from a complicated doodle he was executing. 'Very possibly did. How it could ever be proved is another matter. He freely admits being alone at the place when he first arrived and snowbound for thirty-six hours or so before appearing at Dollaford. The unbolted back door can't be disproved, nor can his statement that the fireplace had already been bricked up.'

'The builders he says he got in might remember if the mortar looked fresh. If they're reasonably sure it didn't, it would put us back to old John Anstey, wouldn't it?'

'You could have got something there. . . . Going back to the allegedly unbolted back door, the wretched cleaning woman who died so inconsiderately must have been responsible. Some chap living rough might have come on the place, seen it looked shut up, and after prospecting moved in for a few comfortable days. Paul arrives late, finds him, and there's a punch-up fatal for the chap. This theory has the advantage of providing the victim and the murder. Yes, I know it was the depth of winter, but there are the hell of a lot of homeless around. Proof or disproof of all these possibilities equally difficult.'

After a pause Toye enquired about their next move. Pollard finished his doodle and threw down a biro.

'Highcastle,' he said. 'There's nothing we can do here at the moment, and Longman & Co. won't have had time to dig up anything yet. Ring the good old Southgate and fix us up there, will you? We've got two possible if not exactly promising leads: Blount the builder and this Venner woman – about anything useful she might have noticed when she started working for Paul. I'll ring Martin Anstey at Randall's to tell him he's likely to be contacted by his uncle in the near future, and ask him to keep in touch.'

123

Chapter 10

When Pollard and Toye went round to Highcastle police station after supper that evening they found Inspector Parkin on duty.

'The Super's away at a family funeral, sir,' he told Pollard, 'so I'm afraid it's a case of making do with me for tonight. The only bit of gen I've got for you is that Paul Anstey was on the line from London a couple of hours ago. He said he'd called to see you at the Yard this morning and would be down here late tonight. Booked himself in at the Southgate, he said. Got his programme all cut and dried for tomorrow. Calling in here early, and then over to Anstey's Farm to see the damage and meet an architect and a chap from a building firm to get an opinion on whether rebuilding's feasible. In the afternoon he's seeing his local solicitor: young Mr Royland, that'll be.'

'He's got drive right enough,' Pollard commented. 'Well, he turned up at the Yard this morning as he said, and we had an extremely interesting session. Here goes . . .'

He talked at length making occasional reference to Toye for the purpose of introducing a second opinion, giving his personal impression of Paul Anstey and the facts he had learnt about his leaving home and his activities up to demobilisation in 1945.

124

'We're having all this looked into,' he told Parkin, 'as well as his post-war life which is likely to be much more important from our point of view, of course. It's an established fact that young Royland's father ran him to earth in February 1961, roughly two months after John Anstey's death. He swears that he had never set foot in this part of the world since leaving the farm in 1934. Now here's the gist of what he told us about his return to it in February '61.'

Parkin listened with concentrated attention, his right elbow on his desk and his chin cupped in his hand. Pollard told him about the tidying up of the house after John Anstey's death by a Dollaford woman who subsequently died at the end of January 1961. About Paul's arrival late one evening, having picked up the key from his solicitor's office but finding the back door unbolted. About the heavy fall of snow overnight which made it impossible to get the car out on the next day, and the time to investigate the building by daylight, a prospecting which showed the urgent need for structural repairs, dilapidation and the fact that the fireplace in the smaller living room had been bricked up. About the decision to have the repairs done as soon as possible and the employment of a firm of builders from Polharbour called Blount. Finally, about local resentment towards him because of his relations with his father, and the difficulty of getting a local woman to keep an eye on the place and make herself useful when he came down for odd weekends. Eventually, through the good offices of the landlord of the Peatcutters, a newcomer to Dollaford, Joan Venner, who also helped at the pub had taken on the job.

'Trying to pin the murder on to his Dad, sir?' Parkin asked after a brief pause.

'No,' Pollard replied. 'Obviously relations between

125

them could hardly have been worse, but I didn't get the slightest hint of that, did you, Toye?'

Toye concurred emphatically.

'On the contrary he produced his own solution. A couple or more chaps living rough, getting into the place, and having a row in which one got his head smashed in.'

'Full of holes as a sieve,' Parkin asserted indignantly. 'Was he fool enough to think it wouldn't strike you, sir, that when the occupier came back he'd have noticed the blocked chimney?'

Pollard laughed.

'He'd got that one lined up ready, too,' he said. 'A matter of some letters on the mat. The owner wouldn't be returning.'

Parkin listened with growing scepticism on his face.

'Stinks like a dead fish, doesn't it?'

'You're right,' Pollard replied, 'but for all that it's bloody difficult to disprove. Two vital witnesses have died. The original cleaning woman, and John Anstey's solicitor, David Royland's father. If those letters ever existed Paul might have passed them on to him, and he might possibly have remembered getting them. As things are we feel that the fireplace is the best thing to work on at the moment. Do you know anything about Polharbour builders called Blount?'

Parkin had heard the name but had no personal knowledge of the firm. Reference to the Yellow Pages showed that it was still in existence and prosperous enough to insert an advertisement of the services it offered.

'We'll go over first thing tomorrow,' Pollard said. 'It's a long shot after twenty-three years but there might still be someone around who worked on the farm roof in '61 and noticed the fireplace. There's another bit of info we could

126

do with. Could you get Polharbour on to digging up anything they can about a family called Venner? A Joan Venner moved to Dollaford in 1961 or thereabouts, and is living there now. Presumably she's the woman working for Paul Anstey since 1961.'

Parkin made a note.

'Anything else we can do, sir?'

'Yes, there's something else I'd like to check up on. You'll remember how Martin Anstey stated that he had written to Paul about coming down on Friday, 15 June and looking in at the farm? He didn't get an answer, and found the place shut up, both on that afternoon and on the following morning when he tried again, and seems to have sparked off that anonymous letter about the arson. I brought Martin's unanswered letter into the conversation with Paul this morning, and was rather struck by his reaction. He seemed completely taken aback and declared that he'd never had a letter from Martin in his life. I had a strong feeling that he was speaking the truth. You had, too, hadn't you, Toye?'

Toye agreed, adding that however big a liar a chap was it was difficult to cover up genuine surprise.

'We know from Maynard Hooper's statement that Paul was down for the weekend of 7 June,' Pollard said. 'Martin's statement was that he had written about a fortnight before going down on 15 June. Of course letters do go astray, but I've got a hunch that I'd like to follow this up.'

'No problem, sir,' Inspector Parkin assured him, making another note. 'We'll get on to the Highcastle postmaster. There'll be a record of which chap was on the Sinnel valley round from about 25 May onwards There can't be all that many letters for the farm, and pretty unpopular with the man on duty when there is one, I reckon, as it means going up there specially.'

127

On the outskirts of Polharbour Toye drew up at a conspicuous white board announcing in black lettering BLOUNTS: BUILDERS AND DECORATORS. Stout double doors opened on to a courtyard and small modern office block. Assorted vehicles and a variety of equipment and materials were housed by a narrow sloping roof running round the enclosing wall of the courtyard. Half a dozen cars were packed outside the main entrance to the office block. Toye waited for a cement mixer to emerge and head for the town, and then drove in and parked the Rover.

'You'd hardly expect to get much from this chap Blount,' he said. 'He must've worked on hundreds of houses in the past twenty-three years.'

'I've often been surprised at the photographic memories builders have,' Pollard replied.

The swing doors of the main entrance opened on to a small reception area where a middle-aged woman sat at a desk. She was comfortably plump with short dark curly hair, gave Pollard and Toye a pleasant smile and asked what she could do for them. In reply Pollard offered her his official card. As she took it her eyebrows went up and she stared at him.

'If he's free we should be glad of a few minutes with the head of the firm,' he told her. He watched a succession of queries run through her mind as she got to her feet and indicated a couple of chairs.

'If you'll just take a seat I'll go and find out,' she said and disappeared down a passage.

As they waited they contemplated photographs of housing presumably erected by Blounts Builders.

'Sound construction, I'd say, but not much of what you'd call character about it,' Toye adjudicated as returning footsteps were audible.

They were escorted to a small business-like office and

greeted by a grey-haired man who had obviously been working in shirtsleeves and had hastily struggled into a coat.

'Good morning, gentlemen,' he said, staring at them. 'Take a seat won't you? Though what I can do for you beats me.'

'Thanks, Mr Blount,' Pollard said as they sat down. 'I'll begin by saying that this call is nothing whatever to do with the running of your firm, but we think you may be able to give us some valuable information to do with the case we're on at the moment which is a local one. We –'

Mr Blount brought a large hand down on his desk with a resounding smack.

'Got it!' he exclaimed. 'Of course, you're on that skeleton affair up at Anstey's Farm. Well, I never!'

'That's right. Mr Paul Anstey has told me that when he inherited the farm after his father died you did some repair work for him. He mentioned the roof.'

'So we did. I remember the job well enough. Shocking state the roof was in. The old gentleman had fair let the house go to rack and ruin.'

'When you were working over there I expect you had a look round the place?'

'Sure. Interesting, these old Crownmoor houses. Long-houses we call 'em. Anstey's had been mucked about, but the original single-storey layout was clear enough.'

'Well, Mr Blount,' Pollard said, 'I want you to think back. Twenty-three years is a long time, but nobody has a clearer picture of a house he's worked on than a builder like yourself.'

'That's true, sir. What is it you want me to call to mind?'

'When were you on the job out at the farm?'

'Well, if 'twas twenty-three years back, that makes it 1961. . . . Summer, it was. I remember that as I had a bit of a breeze with Mr Anstey. He seemed to think I could drop everything and do his roof right away, but that's never been our way, not in this firm. We takes customers as they come, unless there's a real emergency, that is. . . . Say July and a bit on into August.'

'Right. Now can you think of yourself standing in the hall with your back to the front door, looking towards the stairs? What ground floor rooms were there on your right?'

'There was the main living room. A fair-sized room with a couple of windows looking out over the combe.' Mr Blount paused for reflection. 'A big open grate opposite the windows. . . . From the look of things there'd been no redecoration for about thirty or forty years. Proper tatty it was, with bits of the wallpaper coming away. . . . Is this the sort of thing you're wanting, sir?'

'Spot on,' Pollard assured him. 'Go ahead.'

'You went through a door facing the one you'd come in by into the other room on this side. It was quite a bit smaller but in better shape, as if old Mr Anstey'd made more use of it. . . . One window on to the combe and another in the wall opposite the door. A fireplace in the wall on your left as you came, only this one had been bricked up, as you know. Maybe the old gent thought it would be warmer that way. I remember there was one of those paraffin heaters in the corner.'

'Now I needn't tell you, Mr Blount, that we're very interested in that bricked-up fireplace where we found the skeleton. These next questions are very important. Take your time over them, Mr Blount. You're a builder, and would notice things in your own line. Did anything strike you about that fireplace?'

'That it did, sir. A botched-up job it was. The bricks weren't set even and the mortar hadn't been smoothed off with a trowel. I wondered if old Mr Anstey'd done the job himself. Reckon there wasn't much spare cash there.'

There was a fractional silence.

'Would you say that it was a recent job?' Pollard asked.

Mr Blount considered.

''Twas much more recent than anything else that'd been done in the room for many a long day. I'd say the mortar hadn't finished drying out: you can tell from the colour. But I remember thinking somebody'd done the work in one hell of a hurry from the look of it.'

Pollard made a pretence of consulting his notebook.

'Just one other matter,' he said. 'When you were working out at the farm in the summer of 1961, had Mr Anstey found a woman to keep an eye on the place when it was empty, and do a bit of domestic work for him when he came down?'

'That he had,' Mr Blount replied with a wealth of meaning in his tone. 'Proper nosey besom, she was. Tried to push us round, but we soon choked her off and she piped down.'

'In what way was she nosey?' Pollard asked with amusement.

'Always poking about in drawers and cupboards which was none of her business. She was there to clean, and God knows the place needed it. It turned out she'd moved from Polharbour to Dollaford, and I reckon she wasn't missed there.'

'Do you happen to remember her name?' Toye asked, looking up from his note taking.

Mr Blount scowled in the effort of recollection.

'Can't say I do after all this time. . . . Something like Bennett, was it?'

'Venner?' Pollard suggested.

'That's it. Venner. A spinster, she was. I remember one of my chaps saying some fellow'd had a lucky escape.'

After thanking Mr Blount for his co-operation and

warning him that he might possibly be required to give evidence in court at a future date, Pollard and Toye returned to their car and drove to a layby with a view over the town and the harbour. Here they sat and discussed the information they had just gathered.

In Toye's view it did not add much new information as far as the fireplace went. Blount might be prepared to swear that the bricking-up had been a recent job when he first saw it, but it stood out a mile that he couldn't commit himself about whether it had been done before or after Paul's return in February '61, when he was snowbound at the farm for thirty-six hours. And as to its being botched, well that could have been the old chap being ham-fisted, and not used to bricklaying, or Paul working against time.

Pollard conceded Toye's first point, but thought it unlikely that John Anstey was unable to carry out simple maintenance jobs. If not, who had used the tools and mortar and trowels found in the garage? If Paul's account of his past life was anywhere near the truth he hadn't had much opportunity for DIY household maintenance jobs. But on the whole it seemed to him that Blount's evidence suggested Paul rather than his father as the murderer. After some further discussion they agreed that the most useful move was to return to Highcastle, in the hopes that Parkin's approach to the postal authorities had produced the man who normally delivered what mail there was for Anstey's Farm.

On arrival at the police station Pollard was handed a telephone message from Hildebrand Robinson asking him to call back. He showed the slip of paper to Toye and they exchanged glances and made for their temporary office. As he waited for his call to go through he thought with some dissatisfaction about the visit to Blount, Builders and Decorators. It had taken up the best part of the morning and what was there to show for it? Damn all, come to that. Simply that by July – five months after Paul's return – the fireplace was bricked up and the –'

Hildebrand's voice broke in, giving his number.

'Pollard here,' he replied.

'You were out on the trail when I rang, I take it?'

'I was.'

'Any luck?'

'Not really.'

'Well, here's a scrap of encouragement I've managed to run to earth for you. The birth of a girl on 20 May 1917 to Flying Officer John Anstey and Mavis Catterick WRAF at Highbury Nursing Home, SW.10 is officially recorded in the Register of Births. . . . I sense a certain lack of enthusiasm at the news.'

'Wrong sex, unfortunately. But thanks a lot, Hildebrand. Quick work. If one's heading for a dead end the sooner one knows, the better.'

'Want me to track down an adoption, if any?'

Pollard hesitated briefly.

'Yes, go ahead will you? One never knows what bit of gen may come in useful on a job like this.'

'I will be correspondent to command. . . . Moreover I'll let you have a complete copy of the entry in the Register of Births for the record. Press on. End of conversation.'

Pollard put down his own receiver.

'You deduced that the illegitimate Anstey kid was a girl, I take it? Obviously, then, we wash out our bright idea of a man of about forty trying a spot of blackmail on old John and ending up in the chimney.'

They sat in silence for some moments.

'You know,' Pollard said, 'I don't think we should write off this kid of old John's at the drop of a hat. She's half-Anstey, and she could be around here and involved

133

somehow in the general snarl-up. Suppose she turns out to be Joan Venner?'

Toye stared at him in undisguised admiration.

'I hadn't got that far myself,' he said. 'Do you –' His words were lost in a loud knocking on the door.

'Come in!' Pollard shouted.

'Inspector Parkin would be glad if you would spare him a few minutes, sir,' a young constable announced.

As they walked along the corridor Pollard had a sudden irrational hunch that the tide was on the point of turning in this frustrating case. Telling himself not to be an utter fool, as they reached Parkin's door he was pulled up short by the controlled but unmistakable satisfaction on the caller's face.

'The Postmaster's looked up the rosters for the period mid-May to mid-June,' he heard. 'The chap's coming along at two o'clock. In his early fifties, and one of their most reliable men, the PM says. Roy Trend, he's called.'

'Good,' Pollard said. 'Time for some lunch first, too. Can you join us and hear about this morning's non-progress? . . .'

Mr Roy Trend arrived punctually at the police station and was shown into Pollard's temporary office. He gave the impression of brisk competence, and answered the questions put to him without hesitation.

'I see that you were on the Sinnel valley run over the weeks we're interested in,' Pollard said. 'Mid-May to mid-June this year.'

'That's right, sir' I didn't miss a day.'

'Don't you have a day off?' Toye asked.

'You can do, but I'd put in for a bit of overtime this summer. I'm taking the wife on a package holiday to Crete come September. No, I was on every day that month, barring Sunday and the Bank Holidays, of course.'

'And there's just the one delivery each day in the Sinnel valley?' Pollard enquired.

'That's right, sir.'

'Do you often deliver mail to Anstey's Farm, Mr Trend?'

'No, sir, not often. And what there is, is mostly commercial stuff. Catalogues and suchlike. Now and again what I takes to be County Council mail. Rate demands in manila envelopes and so on. It's very rare for there to be what I'd call an ordinary personal sort of letter.'

'Now this is the question we want to put to you, Mr Trend, and we hope you won't think it very unreasonable considering the quantity of mail you must handle every working day. Can you remember delivering what looked like an ordinary personal letter addressed to Mr Paul Anstey at Anstey's Farm during the period mid-May to mid-June this year?'

'No problem, sir. I delivered a letter of that sort on Thursday, 7 June. Good quality white envelope, it was, and addressed by somebody used to writing. What you'd call an educated hand, like.'

'How come you remember that one letter and everything about it so clearly?' Toye asked, the faintest touch of scepticism in his voice.

'The truth was I didn't want to spend the time going up to the farm that day. 'Twas my birthday, see? The wife was laying on a special birthday dinner: a roast with all the trimmings and I wanted to get home on the dot. So when this letter came up in the packet I wasn't any too pleased.'

'I bet you weren't,' Pollard said. 'I hope you got home on time and had a jolly good blow-out. When you went up to the farm did you see anyone about or anything at all unusual?'

'I remember I caught a glimpse of a grey-haired woman

135

in an overall through one of the downstairs windows. A cleaner from the look of her, I thought. It passed through my mind that Mr Anstey must be coming down for the weekend and she was opening the place up for him. She didn't come to the door so I just shoved the letter through the letterbox and turned the van and went off. I'm quite clear about it. I'd swear to it.'

'How long have you been on this delivery round?'

'Near a twelve month, sir. Suits me fine.'

'Had you ever seen anyone around before?'

'Only Mr Anstey once. He came out and spoke very pleasant, and gave me what he said was an out-of-season Christmas box. Nobody else that I can call to mind. . . . Terrible business the place being half burnt down, and nobody caught and charged with starting the fire going. Time they cracked down on these hooligans and vandals good and proper to my way of thinking. And now on the top of that a skeleton found up one of the chimneys. That's the job you've come down from Scotland Yard to do, isn't it sir?'

Pollard greatly gratified Mr Trend by touching on a few unimportant details of the investigation up to date, and finally sent him off with thanks for his help. As he sat waiting for Toye's return he thought with alerted interest about the most significant fact that had emerged in the course of the interview.

After a few minutes Toye returned and sat down facing Pollard. Their eyes met.

'So what?' Pollard asked. 'I'm prepared to accept tentatively that Jo Venner's been working for her half-brother Paul Anstey since he reappeared locally in 1961, whether she's aware of the relationship or not. But is there anything in the situation for us?'

'Nothing much that I can see,' Toye replied. 'It hangs on when she moved to Dollaford, up to a point. But anyway I can't see any woman bashing in a chap's head, getting the corpse up a chimney and then bricking-up the fireplace.'

'It's simply not on,' Pollard agreed. 'All the same I can't help feeling that Venner – if she is John Anstey's kid – somehow comes into the picture. She might know something that would help us over the murder which is what we're supposed to be working on. Suppose that some time before John's death she finds out that he's her father. Illegits now have the legal right to identify their parents. Naturally she feels bitter towards him for casting her off and resentful towards Paul. She probably hasn't registered the late Hugh and certainly not Martin. One can imagine a really embittered woman going to the length of vandalising the grave, and moving to Dollaford to be on the spot to take it out on Paul. But if that was the idea and she planned to burn down the family home which she hadn't been allowed to share, why wait twenty-three years before doing it, working as a char for Paul in the meantime? And yet try to implicate young Martin in the arson as soon as he appears on the scene? We don't know for a fact that she wrote that anonymous letter, but it must have been someone who was at the Peatcutters that Friday night and could identify his car.'

'Seems to me,' Toye said after a fairly lengthy silence, 'that she might have had some sort of hold over Paul.'

'Exactly the idea that hit me in the watches of the night. Remember what Blount called her? A "proper nosey besom, always poking about in drawers and cupboards". Did she somehow get on to the drugs racket and has been blackmailing him ever since?'

'You don't think she was blackmailing him over the murder?'

'All things considered, no,' Pollard said thoughtfully. 'I'm pretty certain the murder and corpse disposal had been carried through – either by John or Paul – before

Paul went into circulation in Dollaford, thirty-six hours or so after he came down. We can check up the exact date on which he picked up the key of the farm from the solicitors' clerk, and with luck the then landlord of the Peatcutters will remember Paul's first appearance. It must have created quite a sensation. But there's the heck of a lot of difference between blackmailing somebody who's handling heroin and somebody who's committed a murder. You'd risk a charge of being an accessory after the fact. A call on Joan Venner's the next item on the programme, I think. Let's go along to Parkin and see if any gen on the Venner family's come through from Polharbour.'

As he spoke, a knock on the door announced the arrival of another constable who handed Pollard a typewritten statement with Inspector Parkin's compliments and a smart salute.

'I was to say the message has just come through over the phone, sir.'

'Thanks,' Pollard said, taking the paper. 'Polharbour it is,' he told Toye as the constable withdrew.

Under the heading 'Information Requested re the Venner Family formerly resident in Polharbour' was a concise report from the Polharbour police.

'The Venner family', it ran, 'was resident in this town from 1947 to 1961. It consisted of three members: Mr George Albert Venner, his wife Kathleen and their adopted daughter Joan. Mr Venner bought a small newsagent's and general stationery business in West Street which they ran themselves. Their daughter Joan had served in the WAAF during the war as a canteen worker, and obtained employment at the Marine Hotel, and later at the Grand Hotel. Mr Venner died in 1960, aged 63, leaving the business to his wife, who sold it and retired with her daughter to a small bungalow on the Sweetbriar Estate. She died in 1959. Miss Joan Venner sold the bungalow and moved to Dollaford in the spring of 1961.

No member of the family was ever in trouble with the Polharbour police, and nothing discreditable is known of any one of them. It appears to have been common knowledge that Miss Joan Venner was an adopted daughter.'

'Looks as though she waited to be on her own before getting even with the Ansteys,' Toye commented. 'Maybe she chanced on her birth certificate put away with her adopted mother's marriage lines.'

Pollard looked at his watch.

'Too late to go over to Dollaford this evening. She works at the Peatcutters,' Paul said. 'They'll be getting going for dinner and the evening bar session. We'll knock off and have a decent meal here ourselves, and go over to call on her tomorrow.'

The Southgate's dining-room was in demand that evening and Pollard and Toye found themselves in close proximity to a party of four, two couples, one of which appeared to be staying overnight with the other while on a motoring tour of the area. Good places for putting up for the night were being discussed, and the Peatcutters Inn at Dollaford was recommended as a very decent pub.

'We've always heard it well spoken of until last week, as a matter of fact,' the touring male guest replied, 'haven't we Jill? Then we ran into some friends who'd put up there for the night recently and they rather put us off. When was it they were there? Three weeks ago, or was it only a fortnight?'

After some argument the couple agreed that the night in question had been Saturday, 16 June.

'Well, anyway,' the man went on, 'everything seemed fine at first. Excellent dinner, boiling hot bathwater, good beds and pleasant bedrooms next to each other –

139

they'd got a couple of young kids with them. All top class until about a quarter past three in the morning when the telephone outside the bar began to ring. It rang and rang and nobody answered it, and the kids woke up and began to cry because they were in a strange room and there was a good old shemozzle. In the end, after ten minutes of it, Roger, the husband and father, got up and went downstairs to answer the thing himself. Of course when he was half way down the bloody phone stopped ringing, of its own accord, I mean. Next morning he complained to the landlord who was most apologetic and said there were no resident staff and his wife was away, and he was frightfully sorry but he must have slept through it. Roger thought it was unbelievable as the family's rooms were on the same floor as the two guest rooms, and it was an old-fashioned sort of phone with a bell like a fire alarm. . . . These places that charge the earth ought to be properly staffed . . .'

At the next table Pollard and Toye sat making their selections from the sweets trolley after lengthy consideration.

Chapter 11

Paul Anstey was coming down the main staircase of the Southgate as Pollard and Toye emerged from breakfasting in the dining-room. He greeted Pollard pleasantly.

'I thought we might meet up here,' he said. 'The only possible pub in the place. Can you spare a few moments, Chief Superintendent?'

They stepped aside in the foyer. Pollard learnt that Martin Anstey had lunched with Paul the day before.

'A jolly nice young chap, my nephew,' Paul said. 'We had a good talk to bring us up to date, and I was a bit taken aback when he said he was taking legal advice about renouncing the ultimate reversion of the farm. He said that having been down and had a look at it he'd decided it was much too far from London for odd weekends. For the foreseeable future he'd be based in London and wanted somewhere much nearer, especially as the girl he's marrying works in London too. Even if rebuilding the farm's practicable after the fire, he wouldn't want to sink any money in it. Well, I said that even if he renounces the reversion of the property I wouldn't stand for him losing out altogether. I'm having a valuation made of what's left of the house and of the site and shall leave him this sum in my Will. I told him we could wash out the prior claim of some future legitimate heir of mine,' Paul added with a bark of laughter.

'Don't you find the farm a bit off the map yourself?' Pollard asked.

'A bit, certainly, but running my own show makes me much more my own master than young Martin is in his paid job. And over and above that the place could be a money-spinner if it was enlarged and modernised and I ever wanted to sell. I've had an offer for it even in its present state.'

'Really?' Pollard enquired, his mind alerted.

'Yea. Hooper. The bloke who runs the Peatcutters Inn at Dollaford and has tarted it up and got it into the Good Food Guide. He thinks the farm has the makings of a small pricey country house hotel. I found a letter from him waiting for me at *Going Places*. But I'm telling him that I'm not selling. I think I'll leave it to Martin eventually. I expect you know the girl he's marrying is Hooper's wife's niece? . . . Mustn't ask how your murder hunt's going, I suppose?'

'The answer to that question's the invariable lemon, I'm afraid. . . . Well, I suppose Inspector Toye and I had better be pushing on, and I expect you've got a tight schedule ahead.'

The meeting broke up amicably. On reaching the privacy of their car Pollard and Toye looked at each other.

'Too good a staging post on the heroin run to give up?' Toye queried.

'Looks like it,' Pollard agreed.

'But surely whoever organises his particular bit of the network would have got it through to him about the carrier being killed and the stuff and the map found on him. The police would have searched the place and discovered the previous consignment. Paul hadn't been down since the beginning of the month.'

'But would the previous consignment still have been there? Isn't this where Venner comes in on our possible blackmailing theory? She'd be known as a link in the chain, somehow informed – perhaps by somebody alerting the local radio station to put out the accident story – and would nip over early the next morning to clear out the cache. The Highcastle chaps would have had a meeting before taking steps. Fortunately Venner would have been in a bit of a hurry and there was that handy projecting nail.'

'We don't know, for a fact, that she's in on the drug racket and is blackmailing Paul,' Toye objected.

'No, we don't, Doubting Thomas,' Pollard retorted. 'I'm theorising in the absence of data, what? But without a theory of some sort of there can't be any action, damn it. And after Paul's determination to restore Anstey's Farm and go on living there at recurring intervals, what about The Case of the Absent Landlord? If Hooper had really got his sights on developing Anstey's Farm into a miniature luxury hotel, burning most of it down was an inspiration. He'd have had to clear the site more or less, anyway.

'Forward to the police station and Parkin. There's just a chance he can get that 3.15 a.m. call traced at the telephone exchange. Meanwhile we go over to Dollaford. While I go to the Peatcutters and ask Maynard Hooper a lot of unnecessary questions, you find the village call box and ring the pub. When somebody answers, say you're so sorry but you've got the wrong number. I'll be able to judge if anyone in the Hooper household could possibly have slept through about fifteen minutes of the bell ringing in the small hours . . . you know I'd get the whale of a kick out of putting Parkin on to clearing up the arson job. He was so decent at having to

143

hand over the skeleton business to us.'

'You think Hooper's more of a priority than Venner?' Toye asked as they drove out of the hotel car park.

'I think we can wash out any idea of finding Venner at home this morning. She'll be over at the farm letting Paul Anstey hear how she saved the situation by clearing out the dump of heroin unless I'm very much mistaken. Quite an expensive bit of information for him perhaps.'

At the police station Inspector Parkin reacted to the possibility of Maynard Hooper being responsible for the fire at Anstey's Farm with keen interest, and undertook to have the early morning telephone call traced as quickly as possible.

'Over to you then,' Pollard said. 'Meanwhile we'll go over to the Peatcutters and find out how much row the bell makes.'

On arrival at Dollaford Toye drove up the lane leading to the pub's car park. As they passed Jo Venner's cottage Pollard pointed out with a grin that it looked shut up, and that the garage was empty with its doors propped open. Outside the inn Toye faded away and Pollard walked up the path to the front door. He knocked loudly and it was flung open by a tall well-built man in shirtsleeves who stared at him enquiringly. At the sight of Pollard's official card comprehension dawned in his face.

'Scotland Yard,' he commented. 'I thought you'd be along at some point, Chief Superintendent. Come inside. We'll go up to our sitting room. My wife's gone over to Polharbour to shop and we shan't be disturbed.'

As they walked along the stone-flagged passage to the foot of the stairs discussing the age of the Peatcutters, Pollard noted a telephone with a coin box in a recess outside the door of the bar. Maynard Hooper led the way to a pleasant fair-sized room, low ceilinged and with oak beams and lattice windows. There was a large television set, a couple of well-filled bookcases and inviting comfortable chairs.

'Take a pew, won't you?' Maynard Hooper said, drawing a couple of chairs forward. 'Not that I can be of much help to you over this rum business of the skeleton at Anstey's Farm. I only took over this pub in '76. Before that I was running the Lobster Pot near Fowey . . . I suppose it's not in order to offer you coffee or anything stronger?'

'Thanks, but no, as I'm on duty,' Pollard replied. 'What I think could be helpful is anything you've picked up from casual chat in your bar about the Anstey family and the farm. Have you gathered that John Anstey ever let the place, for instance? Did he have many visitors that he used to bring along here for a drink? We're interested in anything that could help us identify the skeleton.'

Maynard Hooper settled back in his chair with what struck Pollard as slight but perceptible relaxation.

'I only wish I could produce some helpful pointer,' he said. 'Naturally my wife and I have chewed over the whole thing *ad nauseam* with our friends, but nothing's come up beyond a general impression that John Anstey was an embittered old – hell, there's the bloody phone. I won't be a minute. Whoever it is can call back later . . .'

He went quickly out of the room, Pollard slipped quietly through the door and took a few steps along the passage to what were obviously the family bedrooms. The clamour of the telephone bell reverberated under the low ceilings. It stopped abruptly and Maynard Hooper's voice was audible below. Pollard returned swiftly to his chair in the sitting room, completely satisfied that no one in this part of the house could possibly have slept through a prolonged spell of the racket.

'Wrong number,' Maynard Hooper remarked tersely as he came back into the room. 'Well, as I was saying . . .'

He talked freely about both John and Paul Anstey, making it clear that anything he said about John was based on hearsay. He agreed that the damage to the latter's grave after the funeral seemed a bit out of character in a place like Dollaford, but there might have been an unofficial wake in the pub that night, and somebody who'd had the rough side of old John's tongue at some point might have run amok on his way home. Old Enoch Clement who was the landlord then had been a damn sight too easygoing.

'The place had gone to seed when I bought it in 1976,' Maynard Hooper went on. 'That was one of its attractions actually. I could see the potential here and I like the challenge of taking on a run-down show and making a success of it. Once it's arrived I'm inclined to lose interest.'

'Have you got to that stage over the Peatcutters?' Pollard asked. 'You've obviously made a success of it.'

'Up to a point. I suppose I am beginning to feel I could do with a bit more to bite on. But on the other hand both my wife and I like the village and the neighbourhood immensely and don't want to move. As a matter of fact I've made Paul Anstey an offer for what's left of Anstey's Farm. With the right sort of imaginative rebuilding and enlarging it would make a most attractive country house hotel. He's only got a life interest in it, but when his nephew was down here recently – he's the one who gets the reversion when Paul dies – he said he'd no use for the place and was going to consult a solicitor about refusing the bequest. I wrote to Paul at that travel agency of his, but haven't had an answer yet.'

Pollard agreed that the idea was an interesting one and reverted to the subject of Enoch Clement. Maynard Hooper's reaction was that it might be worthwhile going to see him on the subject of the Ansteys' past history. He had retired to a bungalow on the far side of Polharbour and was still with it all right although getting on a bit, of course. 'Hold on a moment, and I'll jot down his address for you,' he added.

'Thanks,' Pollard said, putting the slip of paper into his notebook. 'And for your help generally, especially for putting us on to this chap.'

Saying that he hoped that Enoch Clement would be more use than he himself had been, Maynard Hooper led the way downstairs.

'Mind going out the back way?' he asked. 'It's quicker if you're making for the car park.'

A path led across the small garden at the rear of the house to a gate in a hedge beyond which was the car park, empty except for the immaculate Rover with Toye sitting decorously at the wheel. On catching sight of him Maynard Hooper stopped abruptly.

'Brought along your chauffeur?' he asked after a fractional pause.

'My colleague, Detective Inspector Toye. He provides general back-up when I'm on a case, including most of the driving. . . . Mr Maynard Hooper, Inspector, landlord of this attractive pub.'

Greetings were exchanged, Toye returned to the driving seat and Pollard got in beside him, thanking Maynard Hooper once again as the Rover began to move off. Glancing back as they turned right at the junction with the main road he saw the landlord standing and watching their departure.

'Obviously jittery,' he commented. 'Not much use to us apart from giving me the address in Polharbour of his predecessor who was here at the time of John Anstey's death. Worth looking up, I thought. Did you pick up anything?'

Toye reported taking a stroll round and having a good

look at Joan Venner's cottage.

'It struck me that she might have heard the pub telephone during the night the farm was fired,' he said, 'but I think it's unlikely. Her cottage isn't in alignment with the Peatcutters. It faces more up the road towards Affacombe. I doubt if the row would have woken her up, anyway.'

At Polharbour a brief call at the police station established that Enoch Clement, former landlord of the Peatcutters at Dollaford was now a widower, comfortably off on a modest standard, and the object of martrimonial designs on the part of the various women who 'did' for him.

'Wasting their time,' the Polharbour Inspector told them. 'The old chap's getting a bit long in the tooth but he's as sly as they come. He's still on the spot, all right. Well worth you looking in on him, Mr Pollard, I'd say.'

They located the bungalow without difficulty. Externally at least it was in impeccable repair, and they walked up the path of a well-kept front garden and pressed a bell push which set off chimes. There was a sound of feet approaching slowly but surely and the door was opened on a chain.

'Who's there?' an elderly and slightly hoarse voice demanded aggressively.

'Detective-Chief Superintendent Pollard and Detective-Inspector Toye of New Scotland Yard, Mr Clement,' Pollard informed him. 'Here's my official card,' he added, passing it through the slit. 'If you'll let us in we'd be glad of a word with you.'

'I'll let you in right enough,' Enoch Clement replied with gusto, rattling the chain and opening the door. 'Talk of the place you chaps are. Watch my stock going up like a rocket when it gets round you've called.'

The door was flung open and they were confronted by a

short tubby figure in an open-necked shirt, old flannel trousers and ancient carpet slippers. Very bright blue eyes sized them up knowingly from a wrinkled russet-brown face.

'This way, gents.'

They followed him to a room at the back of the bungalow overlooking another garden. It was an essentially masculine room with leather-covered armchairs, a massive black marble clock on the mantelpiece, an assertive patterned carpet, and an untidy pile of newspapers on a side table on which an enormous tabby cat was asleep. A bottle of a well-known brand of whisky, another of gin and some glasses occupied another small table which flanked a television set. Enoch Clement took possession of the most comfortable chair without hesitation and indicated two smaller ones to his visitors.

'No need to tell me what's brought you along, gents,' he said, resting his gnarled hands with the outstanding veins of old age on his knees. 'To pump me about the Ansteys, ain't that right?'

'Quite right, Mr Clement,' Pollard replied. 'You've got it in one. You can help us quite a bit, we're sure. When did you take over the Peatcutters at Dollaford?'

'1947. Soon as I was out of the army and 'ad taken a look round. I 'ad a bit o' money put by and I'd always fancied a nice little country pub, and so 'ad the missus.'

'Mr John Anstey was living out at the farm when you arrived in Dollaford?'

'Aye, 'e was. All on 'is own. Come in now an' again for a drink, but us didn't see much of 'im.'

'Did he ever let the farm and go and live somewhere else in your time?'

'That 'e never did. I'd swear to that, I would.'

'Do you know if he had many visitors?'

'I don't ever call to mind 'im bringing in anyone for a

149

drink. I can't say if folk went to see 'im at the farm. There was a woman went out once a week to clean, but she died soon after 'e did, now I comes to think of it.'

'You saw a lot more of Mr Paul Anstey after he'd come back than you ever did of his father, I expect?' Pollard asked.

'That's right. Sorry for 'im, I was, the village being all agin 'im. Mind you, 'e shouldn't 'ave gone off like 'e did and never sent 'is Dad a line, but I reckon there was faults on both sides. An' as to not turnin' up for the funeral, well, 'ow could 'e know 'twas on, bein' out of touch so long?'

'Didn't something unpleasant happen about Mr John Anstey's grave the night after the funeral?' Toye asked.

Enoch Clement met his visitors' eyes squarely.

''Twas the rummest thing that 'appened in all my time at Dollaford, an' it's never been got to the bottom of. Somebody chuckin' the wreaths around. All I can say is nobody went out o' my pub that night tight enough to do such a thing as some 'as 'inted.'

'The solicitors didn't trace Paul Anstey for some time, did they?'

'Not for a month or two. 'E was out workin' for a firm as ran winter sports 'olidays, over in Switzerland, I think 'twas. And when 'e got back I was real sorry for 'im. The woman as worked for 'is Dad 'ad died, like I said, an' no one would go over to lend an 'and in that tumbledown ole place. I can see 'im now comin' into the pub asking if 'e could get a good 'ot meal. Nasty cut 'e'd got right across the fingers of 'is right 'and underneath like, tryin' to open a tin. The wife dressed it for 'un. Snowed up, 'e'd been and couldn't get 'is car out for two days after 'e got down from Lunnon. February 1961, 'twas.'

'But you got someone to work for him, didn't you?' Pollard asked.

'That's right. Woman who was moving over to Dolla-ford from Polharbour 'ere, and 'ad bought the cottage next to Peatcutters. Keeps 'er eye on the farm and does for 'im still when 'e comes down, and works for Maynard Hooper too. Jo Venner's the name. I was glad to do 'im – Paul Anstey I means – a good turn. Mind yew,' the old man gave Pollard and Toye a knowing look, 'maybe I'm a bit soft and a poor judge of character. Take a look at this bit o' newspaper me brother George sent me, thinkin' it might be the same chap, and that I'd be interested. George lived in London – he's been gone ten year now, poor fellow – an' came to the Peatcutters on a visit and 'eard all the gossip about the Ansteys and Paul goin' off inter the blue.'

Hoisting himself to his feet he walked over to one of the side tables, opened a drawer and extracted a folder full of newspaper cuttings. He slowly turned them over and finally extracted a folded sheet of newsprint yellow with age. A paragraph at the bottom had been heavily scored in pencil. Toye moved his chair closer to Pollard's and quickly noted the date of the paper: the *London Evening Gazette* of Monday, 23 November 1949. Under the heading SURPLUS GOVERNMENT STOCK STORE GUTTED BY FIRE a brief paragraph reported that a shop in Notting Hill just opened by two ex-servicemen, Paul Anstey and William Miller, had been completely destroyed by fire during Sunday night. The cause of the fire was unknown and police enquiries were in progress.

'Don't they say as 'istory repeats itself?' Enoch Clement asked. 'That old tumbled down farm's no good to nobody, and now that's burnt, there'll be a bit of insurance money there.'

Concealing his interest, Pollard pointed out that there must be more than one Paul Anstey, and that in any case the local one could not possibly have been responsible for the fire at the farm as he was out of the country at the time.

'He was over in the United States, you know, on business to do with his travel agency.'

Enoch Clement insisted that there were aeroplanes, weren't there, that could whisk you backwards and forwards across the Atlantic Ocean in next to no time? He began to show the fretfulness of the old when crossed, and was clearly getting tired. Pollard assured him that he had been the greatest help, diverted the conversation to the splendid show of roses in the garden and managed to extricate Toye and himself.

On their return to Highcastle police station they found Parkin in a state of unconcealed satisfaction. The manager of the local British Telecom Area had delivered the goods in record time. The operator on duty during the early hours of Sunday, 23 June had been contacted by an agitated woman living in the area who said she'd been ringing a local number for ten minutes but could not get an answer. She knew positively that the house was occupied. The operator asked her to repeat the number and he would try to connect her. When she did so one digit was different. He had pointed this out to her, and she couldn't apologise fast enough, he said. This time her call was answered almost immediately.

'She must have been badly het up about something,' Pollard commented, and went on to give Parkin the gist of his conversation with Maynard Hooper.

'All things considered,' he concluded, 'I think we can take it that Hooper was out of the Peatcutters roughly between three and four o'clock on the morning of Sunday 17 June. It adds up. He wants the farm, or its site anyway, knows that Martin Anstey wants to get shot of any involvement in the place. In the course of conversation it was quite clear that he'd precious little use for Paul, so why not solve the problem by a spot of arson? So all

152

you've got to do, Inspector, is to find concrete proof of Hooper having done the job. How you find it I wouldn't venture to suggest,' he said with a grin.

Parkin grinned back ruefully.

'If it's in order, sir, I'd like to ask what steps you'd take if you were on this arson job?'

'Touché,' Pollard replied. 'Well, the fire is probably the talking point of the year in this area, and especially in Dollaford itself. If anyone in the village had seen Hooper coming or going, or met him up in Sinneldon or in the combe, I feel pretty certain that it would have been reported to you people. If I were sweating over whodunnit I think I'd go over to the farm with a helper who could be a witness and look for material clues. If Paul Anstey or the Venner woman who cleans for him asks what you're doing, you're investigating the arson. As to what kind of material clue you might find, well, good luck to you. People do drop things and make mistakes when they're under stress and –'

He was interrupted by the buzz of the station telephone on Parkin's desk.

'It's a call for you from your office at the Yard, sir,' he told Pollard. 'Will you take it here?'

His caller was Inspector Longman, one of the Yard's most skilled investigators. He had an exceptional flair for tracking down information and had worked with Pollard on a number of cases over the years.

'Not all that much for you I'm afraid, sir,' he said, 'but there it is for what it's worth from all of us working on your case.'

The enquiries at Marlchester College and the Greater London Assurance Company where Paul Anstey had been found a job by his father had been abortive.

'It's so long ago, that's the trouble,' Longman went on. 'We only got the bare record of dates and the teams

153

Anstey had been in from the College, and of course none of the present staff remembers him personally. And the Assurance record was just the dates of his signing on and off. Nothing about his work or conduct not being satisfactory.'

'Did you have any luck over that fire at the government surplus stock place?'

Longman had thought this a more promising lead and gone into it thoroughly. It looked as though Paul Anstey and another man called William Miller had put some money into a shop offering reduced prices for surplus government stock which they had acquired cheaply. Apparently the premises were pretty grotty and had only a short period of their lease to run. During the last Sunday in November 1949 they had been completely gutted by fire and all the stock destroyed. There had been no obvious explanation of how the fire had started and the police had carried out an investigation.

'There was an official record of this,' Longman said, 'stating that no evidence of arson had been found, and that the insurance company had paid up in full.'

Pollard asked when Anstey's trail had been picked up again.

'He applied for a passport early in 1950, but after that nothing seems to have been heard of him until February 1961, except that he renewed his passport in 1960. He was running a winter sports centre in Switzerland, and somebody drew his attention to the Highcastle solicitor's advert. They were trying to contact him about his father's death. Then in 1963 he started his own travel agency, this *Going Places*. Interesting where the capital came from.'

'Pretty obvious,' Pollard replied. 'My guess is that during those years abroad he got into the drugs racket and is still doing very nicely. The Drugs Departments's looking into all that, but meanwhile my problem's the identity

154

of this blasted skeleton. Nothing from the dental enquiry yet?'

'Not so far. But we've cleared up that other matter for you. The adoption, that is. I've got the details. The girl born to Flying Officer John Anstey and Mavis Catterick WRAF on 20 May 1917 was legally adopted on 31 July 1917 by a Mr Hubert Venner and his wife of Cliffhampton. Venner's described as a newsagent.'

'Good,' Pollard said. 'A useful bit of information. Well, press on, Longman, and let your chaps know that I'm particularly interested in any known dubious contacts of Anstey's, especially during the years just before his father's death. Between you you've done a jolly good job of work.'

He rang off and gave Toye the gist of the scanty information that had come through.

When he had finished he sat staring at the wall facing his desk, the surface layer of his mind registering that a noticeboard was hanging crookedly.

'Well,' he said at last, 'we've handed Highcastle the arsonist on a plate and it's up to Parkin to produce the conclusive proof that he dunnit. That handy trickle of heroin clinches Paul Anstey's involvement in the drug racket. But what price the identification of that bloody skeleton and its killer which is our official job? You know, I've got a beastly nagging feeling that we've missed out on something. Overlooked a loose end somewhere.'

Toye, in an attempt to be encouraging, pointed out that Jo Venner had not yet been interviewed.

'Our last lead, as far as I can see at the moment. Anyway, we'd better go and get some lunch.'

As they went into the Southgate's grill room Paul Anstey, who appeared to be just finishing his meal, signalled to Pollard. As they approached he got to his feet.

155

'I thought you'd be interested to hear that young Martin and his girl are coming down tonight for a weekend at the Peatcutters,' he said. 'The idea is a dinner to celebrate the engagement on Saturday night. It fits in rather well, as I've quite a few things to see to down here. Most of the morning went with an architect and a builder out at the farm. They think rebuilding and an enlargement scheme is perfectly feasible and that there won't be any difficulty over getting planning permission. I wanted Martin to know all this before he starts taking any legal steps to renounce the reversion of the place, and now I've got to see the solicitors about the position.'

Pollard expressed polite interest before moving on with Toye to an empty table. They watched Paul Anstey making his way out of the grill room with confident tread, the prosperous business executive in his London clothes, briefcase in hand.

'Why all these unnecessary confidences to a couple of Yard blokes who were grilling you only yesterday in connection with a murder?' he queried, picking up the menu.

Toye replied that being in a dicey situation took some chaps that way. Made them put on a show of feeling safe as houses. Or maybe after twenty-three years the bloke felt that safe.

As was their usual custom in a public dining-room they relaxed over their lunch, the resourceful Toye having acquired a newspaper. Pollard annexed the crossword, leaving him the columns of used cars offered for sale locally. The effect of excellent lamb chops followed by gooseberry pie and cream was restorative. After coffee in one of the lounges Pollard stretched and suggested hitting the road again. Toye folded up the newspaper with alacrity.

'Dollaford?' he asked.

'Sure. Joan Venner. If she's not in her cottage we'll make for Anstey's Farm.'

Chapter 12

On reaching Dollaford they drove past the Peatcutters and on to park outside the church, Pollard remarking that nothing was to be gained by making themselves conspicuous. The past closing time somnolence of a midsummer afternoon had descended on the village and they returned on foot through the deserted street. A glance showed that the door of Jo Venner's garage were propped open and an immaculate mini was visible inside. The front door of the cottage was shut but several windows had been opened. There was no door bell but a narrow slit of a letter-box and an old metal knocker. Toye rapped smartly with this and they waited. After a few seconds' pause footsteps were audible and the door was half-opened. Years of interviewing suspects and witnesses had made Pollard's reactions in the first moment of encounter preternaturally acute. Here he was confronted by a hostile and determined woman and responded by immediately asserting his authority.

'Miss Venner? We're CID officers from New Scotland Yard investigating the murder committed some time ago at Anstey's Farm. Here is my official card. . . . This is Inspector Toye who is my assistant.'

'Can't keep you out, I suppose.'

The voice had a sharp edge. The door opened, and his eyes met a hostile stare from grey ones behind unfashionable spectacles. Straight grey hair was strained relentlessly back and twisted into a bun. Disregarding the frustration and animosity in the face, Pollard noted a good brow and chin, and reflected fleetingly that if life had fallen in more pleasant places Jo Venner could have made quite something of her personal appearance.

'May we come in then, please?' he said, still in an authoritative tone.

Reluctantly she stood to one side, let Pollard and Toye pass and shut the door firmly.

'On the left,' she directed.

The room on the left of the narrow passage was unexpectedly large and gave the impression of money having been spent on it quite freely but with an almost complete lack of taste. There was wall-to-wall carpeting of good quality but of an over-large and assertive design. Some easy chairs were excessively upholstered and there was an outsize television set. The attractive old-fashioned grate was shut in by a massive brass fender polished to a dazzling brilliance, and an oval mirror in a brass frame hung over the mantelpiece and reflected the room. The coloured prints on the walls and the few ornaments were of mass-produced type and books seemed to be entirely lacking.

'Obviously, Miss Venner, you know why we're down in this part of the world and why we've called to see you,' Pollard opened. 'The police are satisfied that the skeleton discovered in one of the chimneys at Anstey's Farm is that of a man who was murdered between 1954 and 1964. We understand that you are a native of Dollaford but moved here from Polharbour early in 1961. We have interviewed Mr Enoch Clement who tells us that you took on part-time employment at the Peatcutters Inn next door. He also told us that through him you undertook occasional part-time domestic work for Mr Paul Anstey who inherited Anstey's Farm on his father's death in December 1960. Are these facts correct?'

Jo Venner, sitting bolt upright in one of the bloated armchairs with her feet firmly planted in front of her, eyed him implacably.

'What you say's true, if that's what you mean.'

'When did you actually start working at Anstey's Farm?'

'A couple of weeks after Paul Anstey got there. End of February 1961. He'd cut his hand quite bad and couldn't do much. Enoch Clement asked me to give the job a trial.'

'What sort of state was the place in when you first saw it?'

'Something dreadful. Damp and cold. Roof leaking. Wallpaper peeling off. Nothing thrown away for a lifetime from the look of it. No repairs done.'

Pollard eyed her thoughtfully, the surface layer of his mind registering the good quality of her clothes and shoes.

'No repairs done,' he repeated. 'Now this is an important question, Miss Venner. Please think back and don't hurry yourself. When you first went to Anstey's Farm did you notice any recent alterations that had been made in the house?'

'Only the bricking off of the chimney in the downstairs room at the end where the police found the skeleton. Paul Anstey said that was new since he left home. He thought his father'd done it for warmth and to save making a fire.'

'Did it look as though it was a very recent job?'

'How was I to know? I'm not a bricklayer. It looked a rough and ready job, that's all I can tell you.'

Pollard turned the conversation to her work at the farm and she became slightly more voluble. It had been the toughest job she'd ever tackled, he learnt. Clearing rubbish to start with, and that went for Mr John Anstey's things and no end of stale stores in the back kitchen, and old papers and cardboard boxes. They'd made bonfires, and the rubbish collectors from Highcastle brought out a van for the big stuff. Then there'd been all the mess of workmen blocking off the kitchen stove and doing things to the drains and the water pipes and repairing the roof.

'Mind you, the money was good,' she concluded with a certain complacency.

'When all those jobs were through what did your work for Mr Anstey consist of?' Pollard asked her.

'He'd phone when he was coming down for a day or two, in time for me to clean round and get in milk and bread and eggs. When he was there I'd do a midday meal if he wanted one, and put things straight after he'd gone.'

'You forwarded his mail, I expect?'

'No, I didn't. There was never anything but circulars and what looked like a rates demand or a letter from the insurance.'

'We're interested, Miss Venner,' Pollard said after a brief pause, 'in a letter addressed to Mr Paul Anstey which the postman on the Sinnel Valley round is prepared to swear that he delivered at Anstey's Farm on Thursday, 7 June. He had a special reason for remembering the delivery and date. The letter was a personal one from Mr Martin Anstey, Mr Paul's nephew, suggesting a call on Friday, 15 June. He got no answer and on arriving found the house shut up. Mr Paul Anstey says no letter was waiting from him when he came down for the weekend of 8 June. What happened to it?'

As he talked he watched Jo Venner intently and saw her stiffen into watchful rigidity.

'The man's made a muddle with delivering a letter somewhere else. Anstey's isn't the only isolated farm in

161

these parts,' she said woodenly.

'Curious,' Pollard commented. 'He described a woman like you in appearance whom he saw working through one of the ground floor windows.'

He let an appreciable silence build up.,

'Miss Venner,' he said quietly, 'when did you find out that Mr John Anstey was your father?'

The shock of the question sent a perceptible spasm through her frame. She moistened her lips.

'That's no bloody business of yours,' she retorted.

'I think it is,' Pollard replied. 'Some curious things have happened which suggested to us from the first that someone in this village had a link with the Anstey family. That affair of the wreaths on your father's grave being thrown around on the night after his funeral, for instance.'

In a split second Jo Venner passed from a state of shock into one of blazing fury.

'All right,' she spat at him. 'I kicked 'em around. I'd found out from my mother's papers that John Anstey was my father. Down in Polharbour people still talked about the Ansteys and what big bugs they'd once been, and how Paul had been to a posh school, and how the Crownmoor Hunt used to meet at the farm. And John Anstey'd just written me off. Paid a hundred pounds a year for my keep through a solicitor till I was fourteen and left school, and not a day longer. And me at a council school. I'm not educated. I don't know anything that gentry know. I made up my mind that when my adopted mother died – she'd always been good to me, so I looked after her till she went – I'd move to Dollaford, right on John Anstey's doorstep and let everybody in the place know how he'd got rid of me, and how I'd been a canteen worker and a slavey in hotels. And so I did move here to Dollaford – too late! Before I'd moved in here the old devil died, back in December 1960. D'you wonder that the night after the funeral I just saw red and ran amok?' she ended on a slightly rising note. 'I hid up in here for all there was no furniture, and when I reckoned folk were in bed and asleep I went out and kicked the wreaths all over the churchyard. Wreaths for the likes of him!'

When the outburst came to an end an oppressive silence built up. Pollard finally broke it.

'Does Paul Anstey know that you are his illegitimate half-sister, Miss Venner?' he asked.

'Paul knows right enough.' The suggestion of an unpleasant smile appeared at the corners of her thin lips. 'He knows.' Her voice began to rise. 'And when I told him, he laughed . . . Yes, *laughed*, till I thought he'd never stop. I can see him now wiping his eyes and saying it was bloody rich. He told me to go and tell the whole of Dollaford if I liked, and what his old devil of a father had done couldn't matter less to him.'

'Does this mean that you had hinted to him that you could make the relationship known in the village?'

'You can't get me on that one, Mr Chief Superintendent whoever you are,' she retorted, 'seeing I never let on. Not to nobody.'

'What made you decide to keep quiet about it?' Toye asked.

His sudden entry into the conversation made her stare at him as if she had forgotten his presence in the room.

'Why, cash. I didn't want local people talking about who I was. What he offered for the job he wanted done. I'm having a better life than I've ever had before. My own place here. Car in the garage. In the swim with the bar work in the Peatcutters. For what I am, small thanks to John Anstey, I'm somebody in this village.'

'But won't this well-paid job of yours go up in smoke like most of Anstey's Farm?' Pollard queried.

'The farm's being rebuilt,' Jo Venner replied with

163

defensive haste. 'Paul had an architect and a builder out there this morning.'

Toye remarked that it would cost a pretty penny bringing out men and materials to such an isolated place.

'I expect now that his nephew Martin Anstey's come back to England for good there'll be more use for the old family home,' Pollard suggested, 'especially as he's marrying the niece of Mr Hooper's wife. And the farm comes to Martin at Paul's death, I understand.'

'Martin Anstey doesn't want anything to do with the place. He's seeing a lawyer about getting out of what his grandfather arranged in his Will. And he's not wanted here, either.'

'Well,' Pollard said, with preliminary signs of making his departure, 'it certainly looks as though somebody local doesn't want anything to do with Martin Anstey. That letter of his to Paul which never turned up, for instance. And there was an unpleasant anonymous letter too, you know, sent to the Highcastle police suggesting that he could be mixed up in the arson. . . . We must be moving on, Inspector. Thank you for your help, Miss Venner.'

She made no attempt to show them out but they heard the key of the front door turn in the lock behind them.

'I'll sit in the back,' Pollard said as they arrived at their car. 'I've simply got to think about where we go from here. If anywhere, that is. On the timing, I don't see how she could have had a hand in the murder, do you?'

As they walked into the reception area of Highcastle police station the duty sergeant came forward and handed Pollard a note from Inspector Parkin.

'Breakthrough,' it said briefly. 'Would you come along to the lab when you get in?'

'My guess is that Hooper left his signature on something when he was firing the place and they missed out on

164

it the first time round,' Pollard commented as they made their way along one of the station's bleak and echoing corridors. In the forensic laboratory a small group was contemplating greatly enlarged photographs of fingerprints.

'Come and take a look, Mr Pollard,' Superintendent Bainbridge invited, an undercurrent of satisfaction in his voice. 'Our chaps here have brought 'em up a treat. This lot were on that slip of paper you gave us that Hooper had written Enoch Clement's address on. And the second set were on and under the handle of one of the empty paraffin cans stacked in the store.'

'Hindsight,' Parkin said ruefully. 'Why the hell didn't we print 'em? We did the couple chucked down behind the house by the broken window where the stuff was poured in, but there were only rubber glove prints on those. He'd begun to be careful at that stage. What on earth made him muck about with one of the empties in the store?'

'Was there any paraffin in the one from the stack of empties that produced the prints?' Pollard asked.

'Say a pint, sir,' one of the technicians told him.

'Hooper was considering trying to buy the farm so he must have prowled around quite a bit. You can't miss the paraffin store if you go anywhere near it: the stink of the stuff seeps out round the door. It might even have put the arson scheme into his head, come to that. Once he'd broken in that night and flashed his torch around he'd have seen some cans in front of the big storage drum. In his place I'd have given them a kick to see if they were full and would save time. Easy to imagine him chucking one that seemed nearly empty on to the stack in the corner. . . . Are you pulling Hooper in now, Super?'

'Some time the day after tomorrow. I've been on the

165

line to the CC who's away till tomorrow night. He'd like a short meeting first.'

Pollard agreed that you couldn't be too careful about possible loose ends when bringing a serious charge against a well-known local. At Superintendent Bainbridge's suggestion they adjourned to his office to discuss the possible involvement of Jo Venner in Paul Anstey's drug-running. With occasional references to Toye's notes Pollard gave the Highcastle men a detailed account of their interview with him.

'Her original idea was obviously blackmail,' he said. 'Pay up, or I'll let the whole village know you're my half-brother sort of line. It must have knocked her for six when she realised that he couldn't care less if she did. But a tough life's made her a realist. He seems to have offered her hefty wages for the minimal work she's being doing for him over the years, and she accepted. I expect she felt she was anyway getting something out of the Ansteys. And to be fair I suppose Paul may have a streak of decency in him and felt she'd had a rotten deal. But on the other hand she may have tumbled to the drug running and been blackmailing him on that. Hence her obvious wish to keep Martin Anstey out of the picture in case he advised Paul to go to the police about it. . . . Well, Super, all this is over to you and the Yard's Drugs Department. You're doing fine. Would that we were over our uncommunicative bloody skeleton.'

A further hour's concentration on the case file failed to suggest any fresh line of investigation. Pollard abruptly pushed the collection of reports aside.

'Look here,' he said, 'we're without a single fresh lead and getting nowhere. It's the length of time. Between twenty and thirty years since the murder, and Paul Anstey off the map from 1934 to 1961. Of course there are records of chaps of the right age reported missing between '54 and

'64 and never traced, but what are the possibilities of linking one of them with John or Paul Anstey at this distance of time? And then there are the chaps who went missing and weren't reported.'

'The dental record might turn up,' Toye suggested, hardly hopefully.

'Even if it does, old man, there'll be the almost impossible job of establishing the Anstey link or – even more hopeless – one with A.N. Other.'

They sat in a depressed silence.

'You're coming round to putting in a report that further investigation is unlikely to lead to an identification?' Toye asked.

Pollard ran his fingers through his hair.

'Well, yes, I suppose I am. I loathe chucking in my hand. Vanity, no doubt.'

'I reckon there's nobody at the Yard these days whose come to it less often than you have.'

'What about your contribution to that, old scout? Look here, we'll give it another twenty-four hours. At the moment I haven't a clue about how best to spend them, but the subconscious does get going overnight sometimes. We'll knock off now. Is there one of your Westerns on at a Highcastle cinema, by any chance?'

Toye admitted having seen in the local paper that a well-publicised film called 'Rustlers' Ranch' was on at the chief Highcastle cinema. Pollard glanced at his watch.

'You'll make the last showing all right,' he said. 'Go along and lose yourself in the thunder of hooves. See you at breakfast. I'm going to have a snack and a stroll round.'

It was a warm still evening and he wandered round Highcastle's historic centre, passing from the surviving sections of the Roman walls and the medieval grandeur of the Cathedral's west front to the stately Georgian dignity of terraces and crescents. All these engaged the surface of his attention but at a deeper level he was conscious of the niggling of the unsolved case. Finally he retraced his steps to the Southgate, dropped into the bar for a drink and made for one of the hotel callboxes to ring his home.

Jane replied, and he heard that the twins were out, having been taken for a supper picnic by the parents of two of their school friends.

'Good,' he said. 'Bless them both, but it's good just to be able to natter on our own.'

Jane agreed.

'Dead end?' she asked. 'I know the intonation when it's apparently that. But darling, quite ninety per cent of them get cleared up by unexpected breakthroughs ultimately.'

'This time it's quite definitely one of the remaining ten per cent and relegated to the "Unsolved" shelf. We've explored every accessible avenue. A skeleton provides valuable data about its late owner's physique but none at all about his human relationships. So . . . Who was it? Who dun it? Why? It's mainly the time factor, of course. We're twenty or thirty or forty years on, so to speak. And concentrating on the victim in this case just doesn't pay off.'

'What about concentrating on Anstey's Farm itself?' Jane suggested after a short silence. 'There's about half of it left, isn't there? I know you've got everything possible out of the fireplace and the chimney, but it's simply impossible to live in a house and not leave any traces at all, even after twenty or thirty years. Oddments that get overlooked. Damage to walls or furniture. Things slipping down between floorboards. . . . A bit far-fetched, perhaps, but people are careless sometimes.'

'Well, it's a possible line of action, anyway. Sorry I'm being such a bore this evening. Give me some news from the home front . . .'

Over breakfast the next morning Pollard and Toye agreed that a night's sleep had done nothing to produce any further ideas in connection with the case, and that a visit to Anstey's Farm was a more attractive prospect than stewing over the case file. They called in to inform the duty sergeant at the police station of their plan for the morning, and set off once again on the now familiar road.

The sight of a dark blue Austin Maestro outside the house was a momentary surprise.

'Builder or architect?' Pollard queried. 'It's not Paul Anstey's lush bus.'

'It's Martin Anstey's,' Toye replied without hesitation. 'The number's in the file.'

'I suppose you were the sort of kid who roamed the streets with a notebook collecting car numbers. . . . Yes, there he is, come out to see who on earth's turned up. Damn! I'll have to think of some convincing reason for being here.'

Martin Anstey came up to the Rover and greeted them.

'I hope we aren't in the way or obliterating clues or anything,' he said. 'Uncle Paul lent us his key. He's tied up with the solicitors this morning. Gemma had an urge to look around the ancestral home.'

'No problem,' Pollard assured him. 'We just want to check up on a few things. Some of the junk in the garage for one.'

'Why, it's Chief Superintendent Pollard and Inspector Toye,' Gemma Ford exclaimed as she arrived at the front door. 'Good morning! If we're in your way we can easily push off. I just wanted to see where Martin's father grew up. Uncle Paul lent us his key. He's got to see his solicitor again this morning about the insurance.'

Pollard reassured her, reflecting as he did so that she

169

looked even more attractive in well-worn slacks and a cotton top than in the London clothes she had been wearing at Martin's flat.

'We've just a few things to check up on,' he said, 'and then we'll be pushing off ourselves.'

'Excuse me, sir,' Toye intervened, coming forward from an inspection of Martin's Maestro. 'Mr Anstey's front nearside tyre's badly down.'

'Hell!' Martin went to look. 'You're dead right. We went over something coming up the ancestral drive, I expect. I'll have to change the wheel.'

'Let Inspector Toye lend a hand,' Pollard said. 'It'll make his day. He's got a car fixation.'

After a brief argument the offer was accepted.

'Super,' Gemma said. 'That'll keep you both happy for a quarter of an hour at least. You'll probably find something else wrong. Mr Pollard, do come up and see some simply marvellous boys' books I've found. Pre-1914 vintage. I'm the book buyer for the children's section of some of the public libraries in the London area.'

They went up the staircase over the hidden cavity unknown to Gemma, and turned right towards the rooms over the kitchen premises. One of these still bore signs of having been a boys' room. The walls had been roughly whitewashed but the shabby paintwork left untouched. The floor was bare boards and the surviving furniture minimal: a much knocked-about and inkstained table, a few upright wooden chairs and a set of shelves with a dozen or so battered volumes lying on them in a desultory fashion. A few more lay open on the table.

'Just look,' Gemma said. 'A couple of bound volumes of that marvellous boys' paper called *Chums*. Tatty, but fairly intact.'

Pollard exclaimed with pleasure.

'We had one at home dating from my father's school

days. As you say, genuine pre-1914 vintage.'

They pulled up a couple of chairs and sat turning over the pages.

'Another world, isn't it?' Gemma commented. 'Red Indians charging . . . boys in small boats on jungle rivers pursued by crocodiles . . . escaped convicts lurking in caves . . . villanous types in cloth caps armed with knuckle dusters . . . here's a prototype of an aeroplane . . .'

'Refreshing,' Pollard said. 'Look at these two boys tied on to a railway track with an equidistant approaching train and rescue party on horseback.'

Gemma returned from a look out of the window.

'They seem to be taking the Maestro to pieces. Look, I'll nip down and make some coffee. We've got a spirit lamp and all the wherewithal in our picnic hamper.'

Left alone, Pollard grinned as he speculated fleetingly on what the AC's reactions would be if he could see how Toye and himself were employed at this particular moment, and turned his attention to the second volume of *Chums*. As he pulled it across the table the back cover fell open. A slightly yellowed official form of some kind and a sheet of tracing paper had been left by someone just inside the book. He glanced at them with casual interest. Suddenly it intensified to a degree at which he was aware of physical discomfort. The form had been filled in with information required by the County Rating Authority at Highcastle. It was dated 28 February 1961 and signed Paul R. Anstey. The sheet of tracing paper was covered with specimens of the signature Paul R Anstey, gaining progressively in unhesitating confidence.

With a swift movement Pollard transferred both the form and the paper to an inner pocket as Gemma's steps were audible in the passage outside.

With an immense effort of concentration he managed

to converse intelligibly with Gemma on contemporary literature for children. Neither of the twins was really literary, he told her, and heard himself describing Rose's preoccupation with art and Andrew's with a future farming career. Finally, at long last, he heard Martin's step on the stairs. The wheel had been changed, they were told, and Inspector Toye had diagnosed and eliminated a longstanding slight tendency of the engine to stall.

'What he doesn't know about cars would go on a postage stamp,' he concluded. 'He asked me to tell you that he's gone along to the garage.'

Five minutes later Pollard joined Toye there and found him ostensibly inspecting some dirty old bottles and their contents. Without comment he thrust the papers at him. Toye studied them slowly and carefully. Finally he looked up, still without speaking.

'Bolt from the blue is an understatement, isn't it?' Pollard said at last.

'How far would you say this takes us?' Toye asked.

'Towards proving that the chap we've accepted as Paul Anstey is actually somebody else? At the present stage it simply suggests a possibility. The first step is to get the lab people at Highcastle to test these papers for their approximate age.'

'But could the bloke who's passing as Paul Anstey possibly have got away with it?' the solid matter-of-fact Toye queried, a stunned note in his voice.

'I'm not prepared to write it off, old man. No one had seen Paul when he turned up after nearly thirty years in 1961, and to begin with his height roughly corresponds with the skeleton's. The vital thing at the moment is not to let the substitution idea leak out.'

Toye glanced at him. He had seen a similar degree of rigidly controlled excitement in Pollard on several memorable occasions in their long professional association. It did not surprise him that they drove back to Highcastle in virtual silence.

On arrival Pollard disappeared into the forensic laboratory. Shortly afterwards he came into the room allotted to them as a temporary office and flung himself down at the desk. Toye looked up from the papers he was rearranging.

'Sorry to be so mute,' Pollard said, 'but I've been thinking like fury. I've come to a conclusion of sorts and want your reactions. This seems to me to be the situation. If the current Paul Anstey isn't the genuine article, the skeleton probably is. The only thing that can establish this beyond doubt is Paul's dental record and it still hasn't been run to earth. I've just been on to the Yard and told them that the skeleton could be Paul Anstey's and they'd better concentrate on getting any dental records available from round here or at Marlchester and in London. They've got the skeleton up there for a meticulous comparison of the mouth with any record that turns up. The only other line of investigation open to us at the moment – apart from those rather ancient fingerprints that the chaps here are working on – is finding out who the bogus Paul Anstey is, the bloke who's been around since 1961 and is most probably the murderer of the real one, alias our skeleton. Well, who the hell is he? All the enquiries about mysterious strangers around at the time have drawn a blank. So, isn't it beginning to look as though the real Paul must have been killed by someone he brought down with him late on that evening in February 1961? Somebody who had a desperately urgent reason for clearing out of London, and who for some reason was able to make the real Paul bring him? Under rugs on the floor at the back of the car, probably.'

Toye who had been following this reasoning with painfully intense concentration, nodded agreement.

173

'Old pal?' he suggested. 'Or somebody who'd got on to Paul's drug dealings and threatened to report them unless he played ball?'

'I think your second suggestion's more convincing than your first,' Pollard said. 'Anyway, here goes.' He put out his hand to the telephone. 'I'm getting on to Records at the Yard, and asking them to find out if any serious crime was committed in or near London towards the end of February 1961 by a chap who managed to get clear and has never been picked up.'

This done, there was little to do but wait. Afterwards Pollard was to tell Jane that this particular afternoon had been about the tensest of his career up to date. It was essential to be on the spot for incoming calls. They filled in time by an unnecessary and rather half-hearted rearrangement of the contents of the case file.

'This'll be Records,' Pollard said when a buzz came through from the switchboard operator. The next moment he drew in his breath sharply.

'God!' he muttered to Toye. 'It's Grainger from the lab. . . . Yes, Pollard here.'

'Well, you old blighter,' came the familiar voice of one of the chief forensic scientists. 'We've got your dental record for you. Up to the bloke's sixteenth or seventeenth year anyway.'

'OK,' Pollard cut in. 'I know what's coming. It's Paul Anstey's record, isn't it? How did you get it?'

'Believe it or not, from the records of the firm of dentists who looked after the teeth of the Marlchester boys in the 1930s when Paul Anstey was there. It's still the same firm, and the son of the man who actually treated Paul is a partner. This old chap was interested in the chart of the skeleton's mouth which we circulated, and it seems to have rung a bell in his mind. It seems that Paul got a cricket ball slam in the mouth and pretty extensive repairs

174

had to be carried out, and a bridge made replacing his four upper incisors supported by gold three-quarter crowns on the canines. Gold inlays and fillings exactly match those on the chart we sent out. Of course he's had subsequent work done on his teeth but we've compared the Marlchester chart with the one we made from the skeleton's mouth, and there's absolutely no doubt the dead chap was Paul Anstey of Marlchester . . .'

Chapter 13

'Conclusive and final', Pollard said when Grainger had rung off. 'We could make an arrest on a charge of impersonation, of course.'

They were still debating the pros and cons of this move when they were rung again by the station's switchboard operator.

'Chief Superintendent Pollard, sir? Will you accept a call from the Records Department at Scotland Yard?'

'Put it through,' Pollard replied tersely. Looking at Toye he mouthed the word 'Records'.

'You're through, sir.'

'Inspector Glyn speaking from Records, sir.'

'Go ahead, Glyn.' Pollard was conscious of his mouth being dry.

He heard that investigation into the unsolved crimes of February 1961 had brought to light a case of robbery with violence involving the death of a wealthy elderly widow living alone in the St John's Wood area. She appeared to have admitted a man to her ground floor flat one afternoon, probably under the impression that he was an official from the electricity board or some similar organisation. She had been found dead on the following day, gagged and tied up in the locked lavatory. Her rings had been removed together with other jewelry and her jewel case was found empty on her bedroom floor. The medical evidence at the inquest established that she had died from shock. In spite of intensive enquiries her murderer had never been traced.

'Odd business when you come to think of it,' Inspector Glyn concluded, 'seeing that they knew the chap's name. It was William Miller.'

'What?' Pollard shouted, causing Toye's pen to skid across a page of his notebook. 'How did they – whoever they were on the job – know his name?'

'Miller'd done two years for a break-in in the middle 1950s, sir, and so his recorded dabs were available. He slipped up over the St John's Wood job on one small point. When he came out of the flat he shut the front door as quiet as he could, of course, by putting the fingers of his right hand under the flap of the letter box and pulling the door towards him. It was a Yale lock and would just have clicked. Only he'd already taken off the rubber gloves he'd been wearing so as not to attract attention if anybody saw him come out.'

'Good God.' Pollard said. 'Whoever vetted the inside of that letter box for dabs ought to have been promoted. . . . Now look here, Glyn, this is top priority. I want those dab prints of Miller's brought down here by a recognised expert who would be qualified to swear that they're identical with a set I've got here. I'll book him in here for tonight. With any luck we'll be making an arrest early tomorrow. Thanks to Records and to you in particular.' When Glyn had rung off he turned to Toye. 'My loose end,' he said. 'I've got a hunch this is it. Miller was Paul Anstey's partner in that shop gutted in a dubious fire in 1949. Remember? Somehow we let him slip out of the picture when Longman unearthed the business. We ought to have checked up on him.'

177

'There's no record of the two of them joining up again,' Toye objected. 'Anstey was out of the country from all accounts and Miller seems to have turned to crime.'

'This is it. He probably got involved in the heroin racket when he was in quod, and discovered that Paul was a moderately big noise in it. Reestablished contact when he came out, and used this knowledge to pressurise Paul to get him out of London after the St John's Wood woman's body was found and he faced a manslaughter charge. The timing fits, doesn't it? Late February 1961.'

Pollard got to his feet abruptly.

'I'm going to get a warrant. You hold the fort here.'

The expert from the Yard arrived three hours later. After comparing the set of William Miller's fingerprints that he had brought with those on the statement signed in Pollard's presence by the alleged Paul Anstey he pronounced them identical. There was no doubt whatever that they had been made by the same person, and he was prepared to swear to this in court if required.

While the expert was being entertained by Pollard to a late supper Toye took himself off, unobtrusively alert for any useful openings that might present themselves. It was a fine evening and the hotel seemed unusually deserted. The presence of a well-known Scotland Yard detective in connection with the sensational events at Anstey's Farm had aroused keen interest among the staff. On returning from the bar Toye had no difficulty in getting into conversation with the night porter at the reception desk.

'Highcastle born and bred, I am,' the man said, 'and I've never known such things happen, not in these parts. More like a film than real life.'

Toye agreed, and went on to express sympathy for Mr Anstey, who, he learnt, was an open-handed gent who always had a pleasant word for you.

178

'Not like some,' the porter commented. 'He's over to the Peatcutters to dinner tonight. His nephew's marrying the landlord's niece. There's a message for him when he gets back, up there on the rack. Bill Harris, as I took over from, said to be sure to let him have it. He's to meet up with a builder over at the farm ten o'clock tomorrow morning. Maybe he's going to rebuild.'

Toye guided the conversation into building costs and the iniquity of current house prices, topics which lasted easily until the appearance of Pollard and the fingerprints expert who had decided to drive back to London rather than spend the night at the Southgate. As soon as he had left Toye passed on the information provided by the night porter.

'Damn good effort on your part, old chap,' Pollard said. 'One of those stunning bonanzas that drop from the sky from time to time . . .' He relapsed into a momentary silence. 'It's gone our way. We'll pull Miller in tonight. When he comes back from Dollaford he'll drive into the garage and we'll pick him up there. No shemozzle in the hotel. But I'm not taking any chances. We'll ask the station for a couple of chaps. Right now. He may get back anytime.'

There was a fair number of guests' cars in the hotel garage, and Toye moved the Rover to a convenient spot near the entrance. Pollard got in beside him, and the reinforcements consisting of Sergeant Ferris and a stalwart constable occupied the rear seat. The characteristic garage smell of petrol, oil and exhaust fumes hung in the air, and it was surprisingly chilly for a summer night. Several cars came in, momentarily flooding the bleak lofty building with light, Toye instantly dismissing them as their number plates became visible. The hands of the clock on the Rover's dashboard moved imperceptibly

179

towards midnight. Suddenly the distant sound of an approaching car was audible. It intensified, and the glare from its headlights swept through the garage entrance.

'Out,' Toye said quietly.

The driver of the Mercedes emerged and stood with his back to the Rover locking his door. Pollard's voice rang out clearly with a note of assured authority.

'William Miller, I charge you with the murder of Paul Robert Anstey . . .'

The shock of the long unfamiliar address produced a split second of immobilisation before William Miller swung round. His arms were gripped and pinioned behind him by Ferris and the constable and he was hustled into the back of the Rover.

The preliminary formalities were completed at the police station as a new day was breaking.

'Is it possible that this really unspeakable type has done one decent thing on arriving at the day of reckoning?' Pollard said as they drove back to the Southgate to snatch a few hours' sleep.

'You mean swearing that Venner was never involved in the drugs racket until she was rung up very early on the morning after the chap was run down and killed and told to clear out the stuff on the stairs? Could it have been done in the time?' Toye asked.

'Just about. The first local news bulletin is at 6.00 a.m. Bainbridge didn't post men on guard at the farm until after eight o'clock the next morning, according to the file.'

'The manager's pretty well speechless with stupefaction and gratitude,' Pollard reported, joining Toye for an early breakfast. 'He didn't know a thing about last night. He's a sensible bloke, reasonably capable of handling the press and the media people, I'd say. They'll be along and starting ringing up any moment now. If we can get away ahead of them, all the better. Martin Anstey must have the facts as quickly as possible.'

Toye, hurriedly masticating bacon and eggs, asked when Highcastle were picking up Hooper.

'About now,' Pollard replied, glancing at his watch. 'We're going to find the Peatcutters decidedly churned up.'

Soon after they slipped out by a back door and managed to get clear as two cars came up the Southgate's front drive at speed. As they drove out to Dollaford along the now familiar road a series of disconnected memories passed through Pollard's mind . . . the path through the woods behind the Priory School at Affacombe high above the Sinnel . . . the first visit to Poldens, Olivia Strode's attractive cottage . . . the first glimpse of Anstey's Farm as he and Jane came down the combe . . .

He pulled himself together and concentrated on his forthcoming interview with Martin Anstey, then abandoned the attempt and decided to play it by ear.

Clearly it was not a normal Saturday morning at Dollaford. A small crowd of villagers had gathered outside the Peatcutters and stood contemplating it with an air of uncertain expectancy. Toye approached briskly and it hurriedly made way. He ran the Rover into the car park behind the inn.

'I'll go on my own,' Pollard told Toye. 'You wait here.'

He went to the back door and knocked. Jo Venner opened it fractionally, and on recognising him flung it wide.

'You've come for me, I suppose?' she said woodenly.

'Come for you? What for? I'm investigating the murder at the farm. Paul Anstey has also been charged with importing and distributing heroin, but he has made a

181

sworn statement that you knew nothing about it. Please go and tell Mr Martin Anstey that I want to speak to him urgently.'

As she seemed incapable of moving Pollard walked past her and along the passage towards the front of the house. As he did so Martin Anstey came quickly down the stairs.

'Superintendent Pollard. Thank God there's somebody here I can talk to. The most ghastly thing has happened. Maynard Hooper's been arrested.'

'I'm afraid,' Pollard said, 'I've more disturbing news for you. Can we talk privately somewhere?'

They went into the bar. It was stuffy, redolent of beer and had not been put in order from the previous evening's opening.

'Briefly, Mr Anstey,' Pollard said as they sat down at one of the small tables, 'at midnight last night we arrested a man called William Miller. Since the end of February 1961 he has successfully passed himself off as your late uncle, Paul Robert Anstey.'

As he spoke he watched a series of reactions pass over Martin Anstey's intelligent face. Bewilderment swiftly gave place to horrified comprehension coupled with incredulity.

'You mean . . ?'

'Yes. The skeleton in the chimney is your uncle's. It has been positively identified through dental records, and William Miller has confessed to the murder. He was on the run having committed another murder in London, and forced your uncle to bring him down here on his first visit after John Anstey's death to take possession of the farm.'

There was a brief silence.

'What hold had this man over Uncle Paul?'

'Your uncle was deeply involved in the drugs racket as

182

early as 1961. . . . Can you take any more, Mr Anstey?'

'Spit everything out for God's sake,' Martin replied desperately.

'Very well. You've registered Joan Venner, presumably? She's your illegitimate aunt, the eldest child of your grandfather, John Anstey, disposed of through adoption soon after she was born. In my opinion she has had an exceedingly raw deal.'

Pollard briefly outlined Joan Venner's life history. Martin Anstey listened in stupefied silence. Finally he got abruptly to his feet.

'At least something can be done about this,' he said and went out of the bar. A few moments later he put his head round the door.

'She's gone back to her cottage. I'm going over.'

Pollard sat on, deep in thought. After some five minutes he began to feel irked by the delay. His eyes wandered round the bar. Suddenly he was alerted by a line of bright lights along one side of the hatch from the kitchen. Keenly observant of detail by nature and his professional experience he knew instantly that the hatch had been opened from the kitchen and that his conversation with Martin Anstey could have been heard by a listener. In a flash he was on his feet and making for the back door. His long strides took him across the lane to Joan Venner's cottage in seconds. He found her back door shut but not locked and walked in.

The sight of a rope hanging limply from the rail at the top of the staircase made his heart miss a beat. He pushed open the kitchen door. Joan Venner, white and tense, sat facing an abnormally composed Martin Anstey across the table.

'You shouldn't've stopped me,' she was saying to him with a sob. 'I'd be a lot better off dead. I've been hating the wrong man twenty years and more and taking twice

183

the wages I should've had off him. And right at the end I knew about the drugs. I wish I'd never been born.'

Pollard sat down beside Martin Anstey.

'What exactly do you mean, Miss Venner, by saying you knew about the drug traffic being run from the farm right at the end?'

His quiet measured tone steadied her. She looked him straight in the face.

'I knew something went on up there. You can't work in a place and keep it clean without noticing that somebody's been about. Like things moved just a bit, or the sink used. . . . But Paul never said anything and I wasn't going to ask. Then very early – just after six – on the morning after that chap was run down on the Polharbour road the phone rang. It was a woman's voice I'd never heard before. She said I was to go at once to the farm, and told me how to find that hollow place in the staircase. If there was any white powder there I was to throw it into the river. And if I wanted to go on living I was never to tell a soul. She said it was a message from Paul and rang off before I could say anything.'

'So you went?' Pollard asked.

'That's right. And did what the woman said.'

There was a pause.

'Was any of the heroin ever kept here, Miss Venner?' Pollard asked.

'No, never. I'd swear it on the Bible. And that I didn't know what was going on till that morning when I got the phone call.'

'William Miller has made a sworn statement saying just that,' Pollard told her.

She stared at him incredulously.

'Yes. Whatever terrible thing he may have done, he at least did the right thing by you in the small hours of this morning. I think it's possible that the Highcastle police

184

will want to interview you and to search this cottage, but if what you say is true you have nothing whatever to worry about.'

'And do remember, Aunt Jo,' Martin Anstey said, 'you've now got a nephew to look after you. I wonder,' he went on, turning to Pollard, 'if Aunt Jo and I could get back to the pub now? We've simply got to keep the place ticking over until we know what's going to happen to that unutterable fool Maynard Hooper.'

The Case of the Skeleton in the Chimney was a gift to the press and the media. It was everything: wildly sensational, grimly macabre, barely credible and crammed with emotive human interest.

Paul Anstey's funeral in Dollaford churchyard got extensive coverage. There was an astonishing reversal of the local attitude to him. Martin Anstey, his wife Gemma, and Paul's half-sister Joan Venner featured as chief mourners. The large crowd attending necessitated police direction of traffic. For the moment the second traumatic local development, Maynard Hooper's arrest on a charge of committing arson at Anstey's Farm, was relegated to an inner page of the *Highcastle Evening News*.

Not long afterwards news of the purchase of the Peatcutters Inn by Mr Martin Anstey was loudly acclaimed in Dollaford and its neighbourhood. Its clientele also learnt with approval that Miss Joan Venner would be in overall charge, assisted by a bar manager from London.

Later in the year it was announced that Crownmoor Conservation Society had accepted Martin Anstey's gift of Anstey's Farm. The Society proposed to restore the building, removing the Victorian accretions, and to open it to the public as a typical Crownmoor long-house.

'A super idea,' Jane Pollard said. She and her husband

185

were having dinner with the Martin Ansteys. 'And jolly generous.'

'Not all that,' Martin said. 'Actually I find myself quite flush. It turns out that Uncle Paul had actually made a Will leaving his property to Dad. So it comes on to me. The probate people are releasing what he had at the time when he was killed, and what is to happen to what Miller took over is "under consideration". It's likely to be, *ad infinitum*, I should think. Anyway, Gemma and I are nicely off, thank you, and I'm honestly glad to be shot of the farm for good and all. . . . And now do tell us what it feels like to have gone up on high, Commander?'

Pollard grinned.

'Dead certain,' he replied, 'that I'm going to be in for the hell of a lot more work.'